GW01191926

The Lady and the Wolf

by

Cassidee Meeks

Fangs, Fur, and Feathers, Book 1

This is a work of fiction. Names, characters, places, and incidents are either the product of the author's imagination or are used fictitiously, and any resemblance to actual persons living or dead, business establishments, events, or locales, is entirely coincidental.

The Lady and the Wolf

COPYRIGHT © 2020 by Cassidee Meeks

All rights reserved. No part of this book may be used or reproduced in any manner whatsoever without written permission of the author or The Wild Rose Press, Inc. except in the case of brief quotations embodied in critical articles or reviews.
Contact Information: info@thewildrosepress.com

Cover Art by *Abigail Owen*

The Wild Rose Press, Inc.
PO Box 708
Adams Basin, NY 14410-0708
Visit us at www.thewildrosepress.com

Publishing History
First Black Rose Edition, 2020
Trade Paperback ISBN 978-1-5092-3134-8
Digital ISBN 978-1-5092-3135-5

Fangs, Fur, and Feathers, Book 1
Published in the United States of America

Gideon snorted, relieved with her response. At least she did not mention finding one. "Darling, if you wanted a beast you needn't look any farther than your bed posts."

Amelia rolled her eyes. "You know very well that is not what I'm referring to."

"As much as it delights me that you imagine me that way, it isn't what I meant either."

She started back toward her home once more but paused to face him again. "Gideon, I've known you almost my entire life. There's no way you could be one of the creatures I'm seeking."

"Why *are* you seeking them?" he demanded. Gideon fell into step next to her as she began heading back over the path she'd taken to get here. It wasn't the first time she'd mentioned the existence of beasts, but it *was* the first time, to his knowledge, that she'd ever attempted to search them out. The thought of her traipsing around alone at night had his heart racing in terror.

Amelia shrugged. "I don't have a reason. I just want to know without a doubt that they really exist."

"Again, why?" He tried to hide the intrigue in his voice.

"Because I believe they do."

"And what were you planning on doing when you met one? You don't have a weapon to defend yourself."

"And how would you know?"

"I know the curves of your body well enough to know there is nothing beneath your dress but bewitching flesh."

Dedication

To my family,
who has been super patient with me
throughout this whole process,
and my editor, Amanda Barnett, who has gone above
and beyond to help me turn this into something I'm
proud to put my name on.
I appreciate everything you've done for me!

Author's Note...

The word Omega has two different meanings for wolves according to the dictionary. I chose the one that is not used as much. I wanted the Omega wolves in this book to be extraordinary. I do hope you like *The Lady and the Wolf.* Until next time...*Cassidee*

Prologue

Cavendash Manor 1810...

Lord Henry Cavendash bolted upright in bed as an impending sense of doom shook him to the core. He immediately turned to his wife and touched his hand to her angelic face. He listened to her breathe for a moment, then shifted his gaze lower. He cupped her soft rounded belly in an effort to feel his unborn child move. His sensitive hearing at first picked up only the sounds of their combined heartbeats before he heard a tiny thump-thump. Henry heaved a relieved sigh. They were fine.

Still filled with concern, he focused his gaze across the room where his young son slept in his crib. He eased from the bed to check on the toddler. Parker—barely four years of age, should have been asleep, but his deep soulful eyes stared up at Henry as if he too could feel the dread creeping through the halls of their home.

Henry lifted the boy and held him against his body, soothing the child as he carried him across the bedroom, and tucked him into the massive bed next to his wife. "Stay with Mama," he instructed softly, before he brushed his lips against his son's forehead and headed for the door.

The servants lived off the Cavendash Estate—in

order to preserve the truth about his family, and to protect them from any dangers that might arise if someone found out their secret. Now he moved through the silent house, searching each and every nook and cranny for the cause of his anxiety. As a hybrid creature capable of shifting his body from a man to beast with a higher than usual body temperature and superior sight, Henry didn't bother donning an evening coat or lighting a lantern. He was comfortable in the dark in only his night clothes, and capable of navigating the halls without their added benefit.

The thundering of hooves over wet ground caught his attention as he began to pass the front entrance—something no human would be able to hear from inside the manor.

Horses screamed in panic, and Henry inhaled a deep fortifying breath. He was confident he could face any predator, but until he knew who his unexpected visitors were, he couldn't change into fur and fangs.

Henry opened the door a fraction to peer through the narrow gap and with any luck observe the impending visitors before they reached his home. Two horses raced across the yard toward his stoop, but the rain pouring from the sky like a widow's tears hid their scents from him. It wasn't until their mounts drew to a heaving halt only a few feet from his front door that Henry finally recognized the people astride the fearful beasts.

"Victor?" Henry threw the door open and it slammed against the wall as he rushed out into the night. He grasped his brother—who barely hung onto the horse's saddle-horn. "You're bleeding! What has happened?"

His brother collapsed into Henry's arms, mumbling as he fell, "Help Rosalie." Henry nodded and helped his brother to the ground, then rushed to help the female from the second horse. Like Victor, Rosalie was bleeding profusely, and her porcelain skin was icy—so unlike a wolf's should be. He wasted no time hauling his brother and sister-in-law into the house.

"Marian!" Henry desperately shouted for his wife's aid, and then immediately returned his attention to his twin and Rosalie. "What the hell happened?"

"We were attacked," gasped Victor, and he coughed roughly. Deep wounds—scored into his chest—gushed with a mixture of rain and fresh blood.

"By whom?" Henry pulled his brother onto the settee, and then hurried to help Victor's wife onto the cushion next to him. She was curled in on herself and clutched a ball of bundled material in her arms—refusing to relax into Henry's gentle grip.

"Rogues," managed Victor hoarsely. "There were too many for me to fight off…" New blood continued to pour from his wounds, and Henry's gaze burned with tears. His brother wouldn't survive this—no one could. Not even with their impressive, fast healing abilities—he'd simply lost too much blood.

"Victor," gasped Henry, nearly choking on the syllables.

His brother coughed again, and fresh blood rushed from his lips when he spoke. "Take her."

"Who?" Henry's gaze darted toward his brother's wife to see a squirming bundle of fair skin and white blonde hair. The infant cried out softly, as if she could sense what was happening, and he nearly groaned in terror. "No…no. You're going to be all right."

Victor shook his head in denial. "She has a brother. We left him behind. It was safer to separate them. The rogues…came for my children."

"Victor, you *can't* leave her. You can't leave me! You're my brother. I can't do this without you."

His twin's gaze, clouded by moisture, looked back at Henry. "Take care of her, brother. Do not let her return home where they will hunt for her."

"She's your daughter. I—"

"She is your daughter now," whispered Rosalie brokenly, tears reflecting in her soft green eyes when she attempted to raise the baby up into Henry's arms.

The soft sound of footsteps behind him let him know his wife and Parker had entered the room, but he couldn't tear his focus away from the horror taking place before him.

"Her name is Amelia," whispered Rosalie.

The life drained from his brother's eyes, just like the blood oozed from his body. He knew he should be doing more, but he could not deter his gaze. His body refused to move. Next to him, Marian carefully took the screaming female from her mother's arms.

"She will be so loved, I promise you," swore Marian.

Henry continued to stare at his brother—unwilling to accept what was happening. A rogue had attacked his brother's pack. They had left their son and were now leaving their daughter as well.

"Take this." Victor held out a crumbled piece of paper. Spots of blood coated the edges, but an address was scrawled across the tattered parchment. Henry took the missive reluctantly into his shaking hands.

"Her brother—don't let her look for him. It isn't

safe."

Blinded by his own tears, Henry nodded as his brother gave one final breath. He fell to his knees next to his brother's prone form and sobbed—his heart shattering. No longer was Henry the spare pretending to be the Cavendash heir. Victor was gone, and Henry was the true Duke—the story he and his fellow wolf— Roderick Rochester had concocted to explain Victor's decision to abandon his title. A lie no longer necessary.

Henry wasn't sure how long he sat there on his knees next to Rosalie and his brother's lifeless bodies, but when he finally rose, he found his small son, his expecting wife, and their new charge all waiting for him in the doorway. The baby was no longer crying but seemed to have a morose look of her own as she stared up at him with big tear stained green eyes.

He rubbed the cuff of his night shirt across his face to dry his tears, and carefully took the infant from his wife's arms. "My sweet Amelia, darling daughter. We will protect you." He nuzzled his nose against her soft cheek and inhaled her scent. Unlike Parker, there was no hint of the wolf that she would become. He frowned and glanced back at his brother. Both of Amelia's parents were wolves just like Henry, and she should've carried the scent of a full-blooded shifter, just like her father, but she smelled human, not unlike Henry's own wife.

"I don't think she carries the wolf trait inside her," whispered Henry softly. "She doesn't have the scent. The curse sometimes skips—"

"No matter, we will raise her as our own, and love her just as much," promised Marian with a soft smile, her cheeks glistening with her heartache.

5

Henry nodded once more. His entire body ached with grief, but he couldn't let it break him. His brother was gone—the only true packmate he'd had, leaving him alone in a bleak world. His gaze fell toward his son, and then toward his wife's rounded belly. He had to protect his family. Rogues had always been a problem, but they'd become increasingly worse in London over the last few years since Roderick—London's true alpha's departure. Soon enough, his friend would have no choice but to come home and deal with them, but tonight it was too late. Tonight, the rogues had taken a piece of Henry's heart.

Chapter One

Outskirts of London 1836…

Gideon Rochester, current duke of Rochester, and the alpha of London's shape-shifter population snarled as he raced through the forest. He was hot on the heels of a blood-thirsty beast that threatened their way of life. The beast managed to stay ahead of his pursuers but was clumsy with blood lust. He could hear his pack mates tearing through the forest, circling their prey in an effort to herd the beast away from the city where unsuspecting humans would see him, and instead into Gideon's path.

Human lives had already been lost and worse—his female kin had begun to disappear as well. None of the missing were a match for a monster high on blood lust and a mind corrupt with darkness, but Gideon and his hunting party were. It was his job to protect the people of London, even the humans—*especially* the humans, like his dear mate Amelia Cavendash. The woman had stolen his heart so many years ago, but she didn't know what he was or the things he'd had to do to protect her and others like her. Humans who knew nothing of the dark, dangerous world that existed around them. For his Melia, Gideon would destroy every single rogue who passed into his territory, including this one. He thought of his beloved as he continued at top speed, gaining ground on the rogue wolf attempting to escape his fate.

His own inner beast growled angrily. It could've been Amelia's blood staining the monster's fur. It could've been Gideon's sisters. He was ashamed that he'd been relieved when he hadn't recognized the rogue's victim, but he would avenge the dead female and any others who had fallen prey to this rogue shape-shifter.

Already the sun was nearly gone from the sky, forcing Gideon to pick up the pace. He'd promised to meet Amelia Tonight, and he had every intention of escorting her through a dance at the blasted ball her brother, Parker, insisted she attend.

First, however, he had a rogue to dispatch.

Gideon's rapid gait took him to where his fellow pack members circled the wolf—forcing the rogue into an opening between several large boulders.

A pitiful howl filled the air—their prey knew there was no escape. The scent of fresh blood hit Gideon like a runaway carriage filled with cobblestones the instant they entered the beast's lair, and guilt once again fed his rage and despair. He'd let his guard down and hadn't been attending to the people that depended on him.

Yet, his beast demanded satisfaction, and until Amelia agreed to be his wife and complete the mating bond, Gideon could think of little else—including the male who'd been quietly terrorizing his territory. He promised himself that he'd do a better job, but as his paws sank into what he thought at first was mud, his heart dropped. *Not mud.* The thick ooze welled up between his toe pads, and his fury rose. *Blood.* It was everywhere, covering the ground as he and his fellow wolves stalked farther into the cavern. As he looked around, the enormity of how many had died shook him to his core.

The number of deaths was appalling. He hadn't realized there were so many. Not just humans but those of his own kind. Now as he looked upon the tragedy and bloodshed before him, Gideon had no words for the carnage.

Mortal men and women as well as children of all shapes and sizes were strewn about the small cavern. Their broken bodies painted the walls and ground with their life-sustaining force. The scent of rotting flesh hit him hard, and his own wolf grew more furious than Gideon had ever been in his entire life. This rogue had to die. Although he was only one wolf, he had wrought so much carnage he could not be saved.

With his pack ready and willing to follow his command, Gideon advanced deeper into the recess of the grotto, carefully navigating the twists of the nature-made formation, until he found the rogue backed up against wall, desperate and snarling viciously like a rabid dog. He faced Gideon and his enforcers in vain, as if he actually stood a chance.

There was no way in hell Gideon would let him live. He lowered his muzzle toward the ground and bared his canines at the rogue. For one who had taken so many lives, a quick death was not just, but it was all Gideon could offer. He took a threatening step toward the snarling shifter and signaled for his packmates to spread out. They took guard near the doorway to keep the beast from escaping, while Gideon's cousins joined him near the wolf. The group faced the rogue and prepared to attack, and as one, they launched their assault, hitting the rogue on all sides, forcing him down onto the ground where his victims lay. It would take hours for the pack to clean up this rogue's mess, but thankfully, it only took minutes for Gideon and his packmates to destroy the former wolf.

"Bloody hell, there are so many bodies," muttered Tristan, no longer in wolf form. He stood next to Gideon and the pack. His gaze circled the rogue's den with reinforced disbelief.

"This is unacceptable," Gideon stated the instant he shifted back into his human form. "I don't understand how this could have gone unnoticed by us. I want immediate updates from now on. I want to know the *moment* someone else goes missing, human or wolf— doesn't matter." He glanced around the cavern, praying he wouldn't recognize any of the poor souls whose lives had been stolen. "You and I have to get to that damned ball. We don't need anyone wondering where we've been."

He motioned for another of his pack mates to step forward. "Get a group in here to clean this up. We can't leave any traces of what happened for the humans to find."

He spun toward the mouth of the cave, and a series of new scents he had been too distracted to detect before, caught his attention. He concentrated on the stench, and then growled—other rogues infected with blood lust had been here. His stomach sank to the tips of his toes. "He didn't act alone…" Gideon swallowed his rage. "Check with the other families, let them know what we've found, and that everyone should be on alert. For now, we need to keep up appearances. If the humans find out, we'll be crucified. We don't want a repeat of what happened to the witches."

****

Edgar was a man on a mission—at least that's what he told himself as he watched the gentry interact with one another around the ballroom dance floor. He had a specific prospect in mind, in order to perfect his plan, but he doubted her family would approve of his arrangement. His chosen bride appeared perfect in every way that mattered, but she was not his. *Yet.* He watched her smile up at her brother, and his blood raged. He wanted no other males in her life, not even her kin. He needed complete control over her.

As he continued to watch his future bride interact with her peers, his anger only burned hotter. She was too free with her attention, and too quick to smile at a friendly face. He would need to break her of those habits. Soon.

His craving for blood continued to grow stronger with each passing moment as he watched her move about the dance floor with various partners, none of which had any right to put their hands on *his* female. The more he watched her touch and be touched by those who thought themselves his peers, the more his need to rip apart each and every insolent sod who had the audacity to babble endlessly to his female. How dare she think to speak to anyone without his permission! The woman belonged to him, and he would have her—regardless of how she or anyone else felt about his intentions.

Edgar's temper boiled over when yet another male approached his mate. His nails pierced the inside of his palms as he clenched his fists. He would like nothing more than to beat the whole lot of them to a bloody pulp, but his cravings didn't end there—he wanted to pierce the flesh of their throats with his fangs and shake them until he felt them go limp in his grip. Blood lust raged throughout his body and mind like a blistering storm, and it took every bit of control he had left over his body to contain the urges that would have him slaughtering everyone in the room. To some extent, it would be a blood bath, and he would bathe in the glory of his strength over their fragile human bodies, but this gathering was not merely constructed of the inferior creatures he'd come to enjoy hunting. He could smell the scent of wolf in the air and knew that he wasn't the only one of his kind in attendance tonight.

Thankfully, Edgar could not be discovered by scent alone—he'd adopted a well-kept secret from his previous victims, and doused himself in a heady musk that would camouflage his scent. So, now, he continued to survey those gathered around him, smiling appropriately when someone greeted him, as if he honestly cared that anyone had seen fit to acknowledge his existence. They thought him beneath them, but Edgar knew better. His wolf demanded violence unlike anything these humans had ever seen in their pathetically short lives, but acting upon those desires would only put Edgar at risk of exposure, and above all else, he needed to remain unseen.

Soon enough he wouldn't have to hide—he'd have his bride, and he'd breed his army of wolves from her. Then there would be no need to pretend he wasn't salivating at the mouth to taste any and everybody he could get his hands on. But not this evening. Tonight, she had no idea what he had planned for her, and she danced with a man Edgar couldn't yet touch.

Just because he could not have his chosen mate this night, did not mean Edgar would not take another to help fortify his numbers. He needed more than one female if he were to succeed. He once again denied his instinct to snatch up his future wife, and instead left the human infested ball room to search out another, one that was not so heavily guarded. His packmates would need mates after all, and a new den as well since the last one had been raided. He just had to make sure the mangy imbeciles didn't murder them all in the process—as they had done before.

Chapter Two

Amelia Cavendash stood behind a curtain seeking what little relief the open French doors granted from the stuffy ballroom. She should have been out on the dance floor—after all she was twenty-six and well into her child-bearing years. Most of her peers considered her to be on the shelf already, but her family still held out hope that she would make a smart match. And yet she preferred the solitude of the balcony away from all the people and their rules. She wasn't her best in crowds or near those she didn't know well. And considering the London Season had just begun, Amelia had many more nights of this torture to endure before she'd be allowed to hide away again.

Not that she spent all her time cooped up inside. She had a long-standing relationship of sorts with her neighbor, a man she'd known since early childhood. At the tender age of eighteen just after her second season, he'd proposed. Not taking him seriously she'd turned him down, but it hadn't dissuaded him. He stuck close, and Amelia had allowed herself to fall into his bed as a result.

Of course, it went completely against every rule her well-meaning mother and society insisted upon, but then Amelia had never been terribly good at following rules. At least not the ones that didn't make sense anyway. It wasn't as if she wasn't careful—she was, and he was the only one she'd ever allowed to bed her, and there was just something about Gideon she couldn't resist.

Amelia nodded a respectful but silent greeting as one of her male peers passed by. His undeniable sneer was odd, but she would not be distracted from her memories of Gideon.

From the moment she'd met him, they'd become instant friends, and as they grew older, it wasn't long before he'd occupied his own space in her heart as well. He had proposed at least once a year since her eighteenth birthday, and she'd been sorely tempted to accept for she did love him. Yet, how could she truly take him seriously? The corkbrain had sworn at the ripe age of fourteen that she would be his wife someday. As a child, the thought of marriage had not been much more than a flitting notion that she would have to consider after coming of age. Having spent a good deal of her last few years trying to adjust to society and the rules of the *Ton*, she'd come to believe Gideon only proposed out of duty, rather than desire—especially after she realized she didn't need to be his wife to reap the benefits of marriage. As it was, he owned the townhouse next to her father's in London as well, and she routinely snuck out to meet him once every other week. Surely something so enjoyable could not be as wrong as people claimed.

However, that particular foppery would soon stop. Amelia had something else in mind to fill her nights.

She'd learned of beasts and creatures of fantasy at a young age when she'd had the good fortune of spotting a young wolf outside her bedroom window one night. She'd crept out and followed the animal into the woods near her home in the country—until she'd lost her way several hours later. Alone and afraid, she'd finally found the wolf—a tiny little thing. It had growled at her but didn't move to attack. After several minutes, it whined, and it seemed to Amelia that it was lost as well. They sat together in the woods long into the night, and she spoke to the wolf as if it could understand her. All be it for no other reason than to feel less alone.

The wolf did indeed seem to understand, and when the dawn broke through the trees it appeared the entire pack had joined them. They surrounded Amelia, and she remembered being terrified, but not a single one of the wolves made a move to hurt her. They nudged her to her feet and led her through the forest back the way she'd come until she heard the distinct sound of her father's panicked voice calling for her. The wolves disappeared after that, and she'd never seen them again, but in that moment, Amelia understood that they were not mere animals. There had been an intelligence in the pack's eyes that she'd never previously seen in other creatures, and it wasn't long before she was old enough to make sense of the whispers she heard among the servants. About how the animals could change their form from human to beast at will.

Amelia was certain she'd discovered such said creatures, and she'd tried to convince her family of their fantastical existence, but they'd gently brushed her tales aside as nothing more than the wild musings of a scared child alone in the dark. She hadn't been allowed to venture alone off the property after that incident, but whether it was because of the threat of wolves or because she'd lost her way, she couldn't be sure.

Amelia knew her parents loved her and meant well, but the entire circumstance had inspired a fertile curiosity that couldn't be denied years later. Though so many of her peers had dismissed her notion as fairytales, she was not as easily convinced. She'd kept an eye out for those rumored to roam the streets and forests at night, but thus far in all her years she'd yet to meet one.

Admittedly, she was a bit blind in her pursuit, as she wasn't entirely certain how she'd recognize a creature in its human form—but Amelia knew she'd be aware if the beast changed into its wolf-shape—at the very least.

Another man approached her for a dance, but she politely rejected his offer. This year her brothers had backed off on the marriage prospects they'd flung at Amelia for so long. She wasn't sure if it was because Gideon, the Duke of Rochester, her neighbor and bed-dalliance was the only man who had ever paid her any mind or because of her age, but she was grateful.

Amelia promised herself she'd dedicate this season to finding at least one beast. She searched for respite, and maybe a glimpse of one of the elusive creatures from the balcony, but when she approached the French doors, she faltered as familiar voices interrupted her thoughts.

"How about Lady Walch? She's a beauty." Gideon's cousin's question gave her pause. Why would he and her bedmate be interested in Evangeline—a blonde witch of a woman, who was currently traipsing around the dance floor with one of her many possible suitors. Amelia nearly rolled her eyes. The girl was barely eighteen and had been proposed to and involved in more scandals than most of the debutants in London.

Thus far she hadn't been caught.

"I told you, I have already met my mate."

Amelia frowned at her lover's response. It was an odd choice of words to describe his future wife. Not to mention he had only ever proposed to *her* as far as she knew, so obviously Gideon couldn't be talking about her. Her heart thumped painfully, and she nearly burst into tears right then and there. It was true she had rejected him—again—only a few weeks ago, but she'd always assumed they had an understanding. The only reason she'd ever turned him down to begin with was because he'd never said the words she'd longed to hear since she'd first fallen in love with him as a young woman on the verge of entering the thralls of her first season. An astounding three years before losing her innocence to him. Not that he knew her reason, and she wasn't about to tell him. She wanted him to say it of his own volition, not because she'd coaxed him.

"Ah, yes, the mystery woman. Will we get to meet your beloved soon?"

"She's here somewhere, I'm certain."

Another painful thump of her heart, and Amelia glanced out from behind the heavy curtain guarding the French doors to see if there was anyone she thought might have caught his interest. It was hard to imagine Gideon with any of the eligible females scattered about, but he'd said it himself that the woman was here.

She couldn't stand to listen to him describe his future wife any longer, and she was most certainly not going to entertain him as a paramour either. It saddened Amelia to think she would no longer enjoy stolen moments in his arms, but she had no control over him. He was technically an eligible duke, and any girl in her right mind would accept his proposal—even if he never said the words.

Stung by his lack of consideration for their relationship, Amelia made her way across the ballroom, carefully avoiding anyone who might think to stop her and entertain notions of when she might get married, as she made her way to her brothers' side. They both stood near the refreshments, entertaining young ladies, along with Amelia's two sisters who were both old enough to be about in society as well. She still had one younger sister at home in the country with her parents, and two more brothers who preferred the gambling hells to a ballroom, but she didn't blame them. If Amelia had been born a man, she wouldn't put herself through this nonsense either.

"Parker, I'm ready to leave," Amelia tugged on the sleeve of her eldest brother's tailcoat. The emerald material paid tribute to the dark-blond-haired, green-eyed male's look. Although women threw themselves at him constantly, he hadn't shown any interest.

"But you haven't even danced with Gideon yet. You *always* dance with Gideon."

He was right. She usually did, but only once during any event to keep the tongues of her peers from wagging. However, since she had arrived not even an hour earlier, and *he* had yet to make his way to her side, she was hoping to avoid him this time—and *every* time from now on.

"I have an awful headache," she pleaded.

"Are you sure? He's making his way toward us now."

Amelia almost whined. "Yes. Please, Parker."

Her brother began to inform the rest of their family

of their departure plans, just as Gideon arrived at her side.

"Ah, here are my lovely neighbors. How are you this evening?"

It wasn't at all proper the way he greeted her and her family, but considering they'd grown up together, none of them minded.

"Not well, I'm afraid. Amelia has a headache," admitted Parker with a frown.

Gideon gave her an odd look. "Oh? I can see her home if you prefer. I'm sure one of my female cousins won't mind chaperoning. There are certainly enough of them in attendance."

"That's all right. I'll return with the carriage after I have taken her home."

Amelia was just about to take the arm her brother offered, when Gideon touched her elbow.

"You won't stay for just one dance?"

Parker paused and looked to her curiously as if awaiting her response.

Amelia would have loved more than anything to say no, but when Gideon looked at her in such a manner, he was so difficult to resist. His dark hair, a rich chocolate brown, was tied back by a leather band. Gideon had never been one to follow society's tips on fashion. And the style he preferred paid homage to his sinfully-fall-into brown eyes. She sighed. "All right." She offered her brother a nod, and he released her into Gideon's care.

Gideon led her onto the dance floor just as the violinist began a slow melody.

"Not feeling well this evening, my love?" His voice was low so no one else would hear his endearment.

"Just a headache," she snipped back, her tone a bit louder.

His grip tightened. "I'm sorry to hear that. Will you be meeting me later tonight?" Again he whispered.

Amelia scowled. "No." At her forceful word some of the other dancers looked their way.

He nodded understandingly. "Maybe next time." His words were meant to be a balm and soothe her, however, he might be a gentleman in the eyes of the *Ton*, but only a black-hearted knave would play this type of game.

She resisted the urge to shove him and demand to know how he could possibly be courting another when he still seemed interested in *her*. It was unfair, and Amelia knew she was being ridiculous for thinking that way. She was the one who'd turned him down, after all. Still, she'd hoped that someday he would confess the words she longed to hear, and she would finally be able to accept his proposal. It seemed now, however, that he would never do so. Not to her anyway. Her heart ached at the thought, but she refused to let it show. He didn't deserve to see how he made her feel. Not anymore.

"Doubtful," she muttered. This time the words were nothing but a faint whisper.

"Is something wrong, Amelia?" Her breath caught for a moment. There was no way he should have heard her comment.

She nearly shivered at the sound of her given name on his lips, but she managed to rein in her response. She wouldn't allow his concerned tone to sway her.

"No. Nothing." Amelia avoided his gaze. She suspected he already knew how deeply he affected her, and how much she admired him, but she wasn't willing to admit it out loud anymore.

"Something's bothering you—I'm not blind. You don't really have a headache, do you?"

She remained silent.

"Were you leaving to avoid me?"

Again, she refused to respond.

"Have I offended you, Amelia? I assure you it was unintentional."

"I'm sure," she replied hotly, still careful to keep her voice low as he had when questioning her.

"Amelia, I need an answer. We have always told each other everything, so what is the matter? Why can't you tell me what has you in such a snit?"

Amelia didn't budge. It killed her not to respond to him, but if he wanted someone else then he wasn't going to get to keep her too. Her heart couldn't endure more pain.

The song ended before she could respond, and albeit grudgingly he led her back to her waiting brother.

"Are you still ready to leave?" asked Parker.

She nodded. "Yes, please."

Gideon wanted to say more, she could tell, but no one else knew about their arrangement, and he couldn't very well demand an answer in front of half the *Ton* without causing a scene.

****

Gideon's heart sank to the soles of his shoes. She'd never looked so angry, not even during their childhood when he'd accidentally destroyed her most prized possession. He'd learned early on that Amelia was not one to sit around brooding—she would retaliate in kind. The woman had a fiery temper, a trait he absolutely adored, but before tonight, she'd never given him a hint when it came to emotional distress.

He racked his brain in an attempt to remember what he could have possibly done to irritate her so, but to no avail. To deny him their private meetings, when he knew for a fact she enjoyed those as much as he did, made little sense. Yet, as he watched his beautiful mate storm off the dance floor, he knew whatever she perceived he'd done to be atrocious. He just wished he had an inkling of what grievous sin he'd committed. Gideon's every instinct begged him to chase after his love, and beseech Amelia to tell him, but to do so would shine attention on her, and he would not put her reputation in peril.

Amelia glanced back, just before she left the room, and he swore he could see pain lingering in her beautiful emerald gaze. His heart hurt to think he might have slighted her somehow, but short of begging Amelia to be his bride right here in front of everyone, he didn't know what else he might do to stop her. He'd been so careful not to give any other female even a moment of his time, and he'd danced his one allotted song with Amelia to assure her that he still wanted her next to him. Nothing he'd done this evening had borne favor with his beloved.

Although the pulse of his heart pounded in his ears, Gideon refused to give in to the panic. He promised himself he'd find out what made her turn on him so readily, and he would make sure it never happened again. Amelia was to be his bride—one day she'd agree to his proposal—he had faith in their relationship. For now, she wanted nothing more than a clandestine affair, and he had resolved to be fine with her request, but it couldn't last forever. When she realized she needed him as much as he needed her, she'd agree to his suit. *She had to*. Until then, he was going to their meeting place, and if she showed up Gideon would demand the answers she'd refused to give him on the dance floor.

Chapter Three

Amelia was grateful to arrive home less than half an hour later, despite a bumpy carriage ride across London. While her father managed the country estate, her eldest brother took charge of the town house. A good situation for everyone involved as her parents had outgrown London and no longer found enjoyment in society. Amelia hoped to join them in a few more years, or possibly sooner with Gideon's bachelorhood ending.

She would never truly escape Gideon of course, as he was their closest neighbor in the country as well. She would have to see him with his wife at events, and it would tear her apart, but there was little she could do about the situation. Especially now that she knew his heart belonged to someone else.

Several hours passed before the rest of her family returned home and saw themselves to bed. Amelia waited until she was certain they were all asleep, and then crept out through her window and down the decorative trellis adorning the side of their townhouse—the same route she always took to meet Gideon. Except now she would use the time she would have otherwise spent in Gideon's arms to seek out the beasts she *knew* existed. Even if her heart ached with sorrow.

Luckily, she had only a short journey before she was far enough away from town to hopefully spot one of the mythical beasts. She wasn't sure what she'd do if she actually found one. Amelia didn't plan to draw attention to herself, but she wanted to observe them—nothing more.

She'd dressed accordingly in a long, dark, hooded cape to lessen the chance of someone seeing her out this late or being accosted by ruffians. The thought of dying for her cause was terrifying and quite possibly not worth the trouble. Yet, now she stood beneath a particularly large tree a few hundred feet from the graveyard where she usually met Gideon. Since she'd made it clear she would not be seeing him again tonight, surely he wouldn't show up. The black-hearted scoundrel most likely rested at home in bed, or considering his new conquest perhaps he shared this time with his fiancée. Her heart hurt to imagine someone else with Gideon, but she knew it had to be true. Why would he have said it if it wasn't so? The man if nothing else, had always been truthful in their conversations. *Or at least she'd thought he had.*

Amelia stared at the few grave markers praying she'd glimpse a blood drinker or one of the shape-shifters she'd heard about. She was certain there were other beasts as well, but those were the two she knew the most about and the ones she was anxious to find.

An hour passed, and she saw nothing. So far, her late-night adventure had been for naught. It would probably be best if she returned home. To stay longer could put her in danger of being discovered by one of her brothers, who often got up quite early. With her mind made up, she started to turn back. Before she could move forward, a long black shadow fell across her path. She squeaked in surprise and prepared to run, but a tall figure stepped out in front of her.

"Amelia?"

She sighed in relief at the sound of Gideon's voice, but then abruptly remembered she was no longer speaking to the man and scowled instead.

"What are you doing out here?"

"I don't think that's any of your concern," she retorted.

"You're completely alone, lurking in a graveyard in the middle of the night. Anything could happen to you! Of course, I'm concerned."

"It's none of your business, Gideon."

He snorted. "We've been lovers for eight years and friends even longer. I consider your well-being my business!"

"None of that matters," she growled.

Gideon froze. She could see his face pale in the moonlight. "I've been courting you from the moment you were old enough. It matters!"

"You're not courting me—you're biding your time until someone better happens by."

"Have you lost your senses?" His eyes glittered furiously. "I did not spend years trying to win your hand just so I could drop it the instant *something better* came along," he snarled.

"Then you put a lot of effort into something you knew wouldn't last."

"Are you mad? I have every intention of making you my wife!"

Amelia groaned. "Can't you just go? You're scaring away the beasts."

"Beasts?" He grew still.

"You know, vampires and shape-shifters? I have

decided I'm going to find one this season."

Gideon snorted, relieved with her response. At least she did not mention finding one. "Darling, if you wanted a beast you needn't look any farther than your bed posts."

Amelia rolled her eyes. "You know very well that is not what I'm referring to."

"As much as it delights me that you imagine me that way, it isn't what I meant either."

She started back toward her home once more but paused to face him again. "Gideon, I've known you almost my entire life. There's no way you could be one of the creatures I'm seeking."

"Why *are* you seeking them?" he demanded. Gideon fell into step next to her as she began heading back over the path she'd taken to get here. It wasn't the first time she'd mentioned the existence of beasts, but it *was* the first time, to his knowledge, that she'd ever attempted to search them out. The thought of her traipsing around alone at night had his heart racing in terror.

Amelia shrugged. "I don't have a reason. I just want to know without a doubt that they really exist."

"Again, why?" He tried to hide the intrigue in his voice.

"Because I believe they do."

"And what were you planning on doing when you met one? You don't have a weapon to defend yourself."

"And how would you know?"

"I know the curves of your body well enough to know there is nothing beneath your dress but bewitching flesh."

"Well, I nev—"

"Ah, but you did, my love."

The pink staining her cheeks was becoming, but he loved when her eyes flashed fire.

"I don't exactly plan on attacking one! I just want to *see* the beast."

"So, if you found one of your mythical creatures out here you wouldn't be hysterical?" His mind filled with possibilities. Maybe he could tell her the truth.

The love of his heart snorted. "I'm more afraid of the *Ton* than I am a night creature."

"Amelia, if these creatures are real, don't you think they'd be *dangerous*?"

"Well I suppose…but I don't mean them any harm. I would hope they'd know that."

"If vampires were real, they'd have you for a midnight snack. And shapeshifters—"

"Yes? What would a shape-shifter do to me?" She sounded almost hopeful.

He studied her for a moment in consideration. "You already know."

"I do?" Amelia's brow furrowed. "You're not making any sense."

"Amelia, *I'm* a shape-shifter, and I make love to you as often as I possibly can. Despite having to do so in secret since you refuse to marry me."

"You're making fun of me," she accused.

"I swear, I'm not. You're right. Creatures are real, and I'm one of them. I promise you."

"But I have never seen you change into— What *do* you change into?"

"A wolf, and no you wouldn't have. It's not something I can do in the full eye of the public. It's a secret, else it wouldn't be a myth. People aren't supposed to know the truth."

"I have seen you sans clothing. I would hope you would trust me to see you change into a wolf. *If* it were true," she pointed out bluntly.

"Maybe if you'd accepted my proposal you would have seen it by now!"

Amelia huffed. "I don't know if you're teasing me because you know I honestly believe they exist or if you're serious—"

"I'm completely serious." He followed up his words with a swear word.

She swallowed. "You've never lied to me before, Gideon…"

"And I'm not going to start now. I told you when we were children that you would be my wife someday. I knew even then because of what I am."

"But…" His beloved's prior bravado seemed to be fraying.

"I need you not to panic. I'm only telling you this because you're the one I'm supposed to be with. That's how I knew. All shape-shifters know when they meet their mate."

"Mate." Amelia swallowed again—this time harder. "I heard you say that word earlier too."

"Where did you hear me say this?"

"At the ball."

"You heard me speaking with my cousin?"

She nodded. "I thought it meant you had met someone else…"

He groaned. "*That's* why you were acting so strangely!" He wanted to shout with relief. "No, my love. I was speaking of you."

"Then you haven't met anyone you want more?"

He chuckled. "I just admitted that I am a creature able to change my form into a wolf, and you're more concerned with whether or not I met another woman?"

"Well, creature or not, I wouldn't just let anyone in my bed, and I wasn't about to continue with you if you were with someone else!"

"You're standing there aware of my true nature, knowing fully well that I have been a shifter the entire time we have known each other, and you're not afraid?"

"Why should I be afraid? I'm more befogged than frightened, and possibly in a bit of a miff because you never said anything before now, and dare I say curious, but not afraid. If you're telling the truth, then all this time I've been close to someone that everyone assured me did not exist, and everything I suspected is in fact true! Besides, I love—" she clapped her hands over her mouth.

"Amelia."

She took off at a fast jog toward her house.

"Wait!"

"My brothers will notice I'm missing."

"Please!" Gideon didn't know what he would do if she didn't oblige him in his plea.

Amelia froze. Gideon sounded so desperate, she couldn't ignore his entreaty.

He caught up with her easily. "Say it."

"Say what," she feigned innocently.

"I need you to say it…please."

"I'm sure I don't know what you're talking about," she persisted.

Gideon sighed. "Don't be afraid of me, Melia. I would never hurt you."

"I'm not afraid."

"Then say it."

She grimaced. "I like you, Gideon. A lot. I have for a long while. Is that what you want to hear?"

"You know it's not, but it's better than nothing."

Amelia was more befogged than ever. What reason could he possibly have for wanting to hear her admit her true feelings, when he hadn't yet admitted his? What difference did it make?

"Have I always been the only one?" She needed to know. Still unsure if he was telling the truth about his ability to shift at will.

"Always." He glanced toward her house, just far enough away that no one would see them should he pull her into his arms. "Do you hate me now that you know what I am?"

Amelia softened inside at his question. "Why would I hate you? You're still Gideon. It doesn't change who you are, right? You're not going to change into a wolf and eat me, are you?"

He grinned mischievously. "I don't need to be a wolf to dine on your flesh."

Her cheeks heated significantly at his provocative words, but before she could respond, he reached out, grasped her upper arms, and pulled her closer.

"Am I still allowed to kiss you, or does this change things between us?"

Amelia bit her bottom lip in anticipation. "I don't see why it would."

Gideon pulled her the rest of the way toward his body and into his arms—where he kissed her soundly as if it was the first time all over again.

She moaned as the liquid fire she'd come to expect flooded her body at the mere touch of his lips. Her entire being flamed under his grasp, and she melted into his touch, needing to feel more of him against her flesh.

His hands dropped to her hips, and he tugged her against him until she could feel the length of him straining against his breeches, wanting her.

"We don't have time for this," she gasped.

"Maybe not, but we have a few moments." He pressed a series of soft kisses to her cheeks and forehead as his hands traced the contours of her body.

"I suppose you aren't going to let me hunt creatures, are you?" she whispered solemnly.

"Hunt me." He growled his command.

She laughed breathlessly. "And how does one hunt you, Gideon?"

"It's easy," he whispered, his lips brushing her throat as he spoke. "You need only take off your clothes and call my name."

"How will I know if you've heard me?"

"Say it as loud as you can. I'm never far from you, my love."

"Never?"

"I make it a point to plan my entire day around your schedule."

"But how do you know my schedule?" she gasped.

"I'm friends with your brothers, remember?"

"Well of course, but they don't know about us."

"Maybe not all, but they do know I intend to marry you. I told them years ago."

"Then you were serious about those proposals."

Gideon stopped abruptly. "Yes, I told you already. Do you still think I wasn't?"

She shrugged, dazed from his magical kisses. "You first asked when we were so young, how was I to know you truly meant what you said?"

"Maybe, because I couldn't keep my hands off you as we grew older? I started pursuing you the instant you made your debut. I've made love to you to in at least ten gardens, several private studies, a few wine cellars, a couple of servant staircases, and multiple carriages. How could you think I didn't mean my proposals? Do you honestly think I'm the sort of cad to seduce you with no intentions?"

"Well...no, but I didn't consider that you might actually *want* to marry me. I thought it was simply because you enjoyed other *aspects* of our relationship." She smirked.

Gideon chuckled. "No, my love. I befriended you the instant we met. In all fairness I proposed to you first *before* I seduced you. A gentleman would have waited, but I can't keep my hands off you. You're much too tempting. Wolves often have a hard time resisting their mates."

"What is a mate? In your terms."

"Exactly as it sounds. You are...my everything. Wolves can bed whomever they want, but the moment they meet the person they're meant to be with interest in anyone else ceases. For us it's immediate. We don't have to court someone to know if we're compatible— our instincts tell us we have found our other half. We only get one mate throughout our entire lives."

"And you knew at fourteen when we met that I was the mate for you?"

He nodded. "It wasn't sexual, yet, but the older we got the physical connection matured as well."

"Hence why we were such good friends," she summarized. "What was it like when we were kids?"

"I want to explain it all to you and I will. But not out here, not in the middle of the night. Marry me, Amelia, and I'll answer every question you have. Please, I'm completely serious. I want you to be my wife. I'll keep you safe, always. I swear."

She inhaled sharply. He still hadn't said the words she wanted so badly to hear.

"No, Gideon. I'm sorry."

"Because of what I am?"

She shook her head and pulled away from his grasp.

"Then why? I have already proven that I'm serious. What do you need from me?"

Amelia continued toward her house. She refused to say. He had to come to it on his own or it wouldn't mean anything.

"Do you even want to marry me? Do you enjoy being with me," he asked, as he kept pace beside her.

"Don't worry, Gideon. I wouldn't marry anyone but you."

"Then why do you keep saying no? What am I doing wrong?"

"You're not doing anything wrong—"

"But I'm not doing *something right* either, or you would have said yes!"

Amelia sighed. "It'll come to you," she promised. At least she hoped it would.

He groaned. "I don't know what more I can do. I have proposed to you in front of your family, I make sure to dance with you at every event. I leave and arrive in London the same time you do to make sure we're not apart for long. Is it…do I not please you?"

Amelia almost tripped. "Yes, Gideon."

"Well, I usually consider myself rather intelligent, but for the life of me I can't figure out what's keeping you from agreeing."

She paused just before they reached the gate leading to the garden outside her house and lowered her voice.

"If I tell you it won't mean as much."

"I know you want to be with me, and you know I want to be with you. That's all that should matter! I'm a duke. I have plenty of finances to support you, and I have the title, as well as the support of your family. What's missing?"

"Goodnight, Gideon." She went up on her tiptoes and kissed his cheek before opening the gate.

"Wait." He grasped her wrist, closed the distance between them, and kissed her fully on the mouth.

The heat of his mouth nearly made her forget why she kept refusing his hand to begin with.

"I'm going to figure it out, Amelia. I swear. Don't ever think I don't want you. I will spend the rest of my life trying to earn your hand in marriage. I'll do whatever it takes. Just…you're not a wolf so it doesn't affect you the same way, but please promise me you won't give up and accept another?"

Amelia smiled softly. *That* she could do. "Creature or not, Gideon, as I already told you, you're the only one I'll ever marry. I swear."

She knew he watched her make her way through the hedges and into the garden to climb the trellis up to her room. She could feel his gaze on her as she closed the window. Now, Amelia watched *him* turn toward the street and make his way home. She wouldn't be able to see him enter his own estate, but she knew he wasn't far away.

The light from a candle flickered behind her, and she spun to find Parker in the doorway—glowering at her. "*Please* tell me you weren't meeting someone."

"I wasn't," she swore honestly. It was technically the truth. She hadn't intended to meet Gideon near the cemetery.

"Tell me you're not having secret trysts in the garden at night."

She hesitated, but she'd never been able to successfully lie to her family. Even now, she knew he'd recognize it if she denied the truth. Amelia was not at all sure how she could get out of answering her brother.

He swore out loud. "Amelia!"

"I'm not a child, Parker, and it's not as if I need to worry about marriageable prospects!"

"I know it doesn't seem like it, certainly not to the *Ton*, but you're still young, Amelia."

Amelia frowned. "Only fortune hunters would marry me at my age."

"I know Mother and Papa haven't always told you everything, but you can't just go about hiking up your skirts for every rake who looks your way!"

"What is that supposed to mean? What haven't they told me?"

"It doesn't matter. This ends tonight."

"No."

"No?" He barked the question.

"I said no. Send me back to the country if you must, but I'm done pretending I'm interested in making a match. I have spent nine years playing the part." And until Gideon came up to snuff, she'd rather not be on display.

"Whether you make a match or not matters little." He took a step toward her.

Parker sniffed the air around her as if he were a dog, and his eyes widened.

"It was Gideon!"

"What?"

"I have been so stupid! I thought it was because he was always nearby. *He's* the one you've been meeting! Don't bother lying—I can smell him on you."

"Excuse me! You can *smell* him?" She swallowed. "Are you mad?"

"*You're* a female, and *we're* not even full-blooded, so you wouldn't know what I'm talking about, but Gideon, hah, he *knows* better!"

"Parker, you're not making any sense."

"It's all going to make perfect sense in just a moment." He grabbed her hand and half dragged her out of the room and down the stairs.

"What's going on?" Hadley, her second eldest brother, demanded as they passed his open bedroom door.

"Gideon," snarled Parker.

Hadley's eyes grew round, and he too sniffed the air as she passed by. "But...but...they're not even betrothed!"

"Will you stop? You both are acting addlepated!"

"Come on, Amelia." Parker pulled her into the foyer and then out the door, not even waiting for Hadley to catch up, though she knew he followed as well.

Within minutes they stood at the entryway of Gideon's home, and Parker lifted the knocker to pound on the thick wooden door.

It opened within minutes, but it wasn't Gideon's servant that answered. It was Gideon himself—still completely dressed as if he'd been expecting her. At first he seemed confused to see all of them, but then what looked like awareness filled his gaze. He stepped back to let them in and closed the door firmly behind them.

"Before you say anything—" he began, as if he already knew why they'd arrived at his door in the dead of night.

Gideon didn't get a chance to finish his sentence. Parker released his grip on Amelia and punched him in the face.

Chapter Four

"Parker," Amelia cried. "What is *wrong* with you?"

"Don't bother denying your trysts with Gideon. As I said, I can smell him on you."

Gideon froze, his hand inches from his abused face. "You said *smell*?"

Parker rolled his eyes. "I realize we're only half-blooded, and a full-blooded shifter like you can't scent us as easily, but even so you can't just seduce a duke's daughter without consequences! You have to marry her!"

"Yes," agreed Gideon instantly. "Absolutely. Immediately."

Parker looked stunned. "Yes?"

"As soon as possible," agreed Gideon.

"No," growled Amelia.

All three men stared at her.

"What?" gasped Parker.

"I said, no!"

Gideon sighed. "I have been proposing to her at least three times a year if not more. She won't accept. You heard her tell me no yourself, just last year."

"And you seduced her anyway." Parker's words ended in a snarl.

"Not intentionally! You said you could scent me. Does that mean you—"

"Half, just as I said," admitted Parker reluctantly.

"What does that mean?" Amelia's tone went up an octave.

"Does she know about you?" whispered Hadley.

Gideon nodded.

"It means," began Hadley carefully. "That Mother and Papa didn't tell you because unless you meet your mate it doesn't matter."

"That word." Amelia glanced sharply at Gideon. "*He* used that word too."

Parker groaned. "Are you sure, Gideon?"

"From the first time I saw her."

Amelia's brother nodded as if that explained everything, but she was more befuddled than ever. "Explain. *Now*."

"Mother is human. Papa is…not."

"What?" Amelia's shock at his words turned into a shiver of ice.

"Papa is a beast like the ones you keep talking about. We're half-blooded. Females don't usually get any of the perks unless they meet their mate. Gideon can unlock the change after he binds you, but until then you're as human as Mother."

"But you're not?"

Parker shook his head. "No. Males get all the same perks as a full-blooded creature like Gideon."

"You said you smelled him—shouldn't Papa have smelled him a long time ago?"

Parker spun on Gideon.

Gideon sighed. "Go ahead, plant me another facer."

"How long?" demanded Parker.

Amelia clamped her mouth shut.

"Gideon," snarled her brother.

"Eight years roughly."

Parker swore and punched Gideon again.

Gideon didn't even try to duck.

"Stop," screamed Amelia. "It's not like I told him no!"

"You should have!"

"I...couldn't." Amelia frowned. "I didn't want to."

Hadley groaned. "It's the heat. She can't control it any more than he can. Stop hitting him, Parker."

"What's a heat?"

"It's what the female experiences when she meets her mate. You just didn't recognize it because you're not a full-blood, Amelia," explained Hadley gently. "It's not your fault, and it's not Gideon's fault. It's just the way it is."

Amelia felt her heart sink. "So, this is just because of what we are?"

"No!" Gideon leaped toward her. "Don't think that, even for a moment. All it does is magnify the attraction we already have, but it doesn't invent the emotion. The connection we share between us was there when we were children. Remember? We were friends."

"But you only wanted to be my friend because I'm your mate—not because of who I am as a person."

"I swear to you it isn't like that at all!" Gideon grasped her upper arms gently, ignoring Parker's frown. "The mating doesn't create the bond—it only strengthens the previous link. We already had something—that's what makes us mates."

"I was so stupid! I should have realized when you were the only one who was interested in me that there's something wrong with me. You only want me because of this...this...whatever *this* is!"

"Amelia, there's nothing wrong with you! No one seemed interested because of me! I paid them off, warned them away, bribed them, whatever I had to do to make them stay away from you. I made it clear that I intended to marry you. What we are does not control our relationship."

She sniffed and swiped at the tears streaming down her face. "I want to go home."

"Amelia—" began Gideon softly.

"I want to go home." She yanked the door open and stomped outside without stopping to see if her brothers followed. Gideon must have made an effort to, but she heard Parker tell him to stay. After that she didn't know if anything else was said, because she was halfway home with Hadley keeping pace at her side.

He didn't say anything as they entered the house, even though the rest of her siblings were awake and waiting in the foyer. But upon seeing her tears they remained silent.

Amelia was thankful. She made it to her room, undressed, and was in bed as fast as she possibly could be, and she didn't want anyone checking in on her. She had no desire to talk to anyone about this evening's events. Her heart ached because of the betrayal enacted by Gideon and her parents.

****

Edgar was in a rare mood as he thrust the female shifter into the disheveled hovel he'd been forced to rent. Thanks to the wolves who thought themselves above him, he'd been forced to relocate his pack of rogues, and he wasn't pleased. Their new den wasn't much more than a hole in the wall as far as he was concerned, but he couldn't exactly have them living in his own house where anyone might spot the mangy beasts. He did well to hide his own nature from unsuspecting neighbors. He couldn't have the boisterous killers traipsing in and out spoiling his plans. At least, not until he could take out London's alpha.

The new house wasn't much better than the squalor they'd been living in when he found them, but it hid the scent of their voracious appetites from the rest of the wolves in London. The scent of blood and the sounds of their victims' screams was easily overpowered by the existence of the Thames River right outside their door. It would've made for an easy dumping ground *if* the crackbrains had been smart enough to dispose of their leftovers.

Edgar had ordered them to get rid of the bodies a hundred times, but they seldom followed his commands—one of *many* reasons why he needed a mate of his own. His own offspring would do as he instructed without question—of that he was certain. Until then, he was stuck with this uncouth lot.

His gaze traveled around the room, and he wrinkled his nose in disgust. He almost felt bad for the new female. He'd plucked her from an alley not far from her own home and knocked her unconscious so he could haul her back without worry of anyone discovering them. Except now that he saw her in the same room with the others, he almost wished he'd locked her in his wine cellar instead. These bastards wouldn't know how to treat her even if Edgar explained in great exaggerated detail.

There was too much risk of her being discovered if he kept her with him. At least this way, if she were found it would be others who would be blamed, and they would take the fall for his recent indiscretions, just like the last one had.

The female moaned as she awoke on the floor in front of him, and Edgar was almost disappointed that she didn't immediately attack him. He liked when they fought back. The last one had been a fighter, and he'd thoroughly enjoyed her, but the rogues hadn't been able to handle the woman. She'd killed one of his men, and they'd responded by ending her young life. *Such a tragedy*. She would've made a fine mother for his offspring. Instead, her body lay undisturbed in the back room where he'd ordered them to deposit her remains. He wasn't yet sure if he should dump her body in the river or leave her in the woods to throw any who might be hunting him off his scent. Either way would attract attention, but so long as it was just a human, he wouldn't worry too much. They were easily dealt with.

"Don't kill this one," snarled Edgar as the female crawled away from him toward a female abducted earlier in the week. She was chained and hardly conscious herself, but she hugged the new female to her body protectively, and together they huddled in the corner—away from the rogues who currently sat consuming their latest victim like starved animals. "Tie her up," he snapped, when the rogues failed to respond to his command.

One of the rogues, more coherent than the others, grudgingly abandoned his meal to contain the female, then rushed back to the table as if afraid the others would devour his portion.

Edgar rolled his eyes. He had a new plan—one that wouldn't involve the rogues. He only needed them for a bit longer, but once he had his own chosen mate in hand, they'd no longer be necessary. If nothing else, they made good guard dogs. Not a single human who'd come to investigate their den had lived to tell about a myth come true.

Chapter Five

It had been an incredibly long week. Filled with balls, luncheons, calls, musicals, and dress fittings Amelia had refused to go to, as well as refusing to leave her room. Seven days of ignoring her brothers, sisters, and especially Gideon. She ate occasionally, but other than her lady's maid she refused to speak to anyone. She would have liked to have gone back to the country with her parents and two younger sisters, but she knew Parker would still disagree, so she stayed in her room.

On the eighth day, her bedroom door opened and hit the wall with a loud thump. She offered Parker an icy stare when he entered her room without permission.

He met her chilly reception with a steely gaze of his own.

At least she was dressed today, though she'd refused to pin her hair up. "What do you want?"

"Gideon is in the study."

"So?"

"So, we have bigger problems to worry about. Stop sulking and go speak to him."

"No."

"NOW, Amelia!"

"NO!"

"You're being ridiculous."

"You're being insensitive," she retorted.

"I *know*…I know…" He sighed. "I understand, and

I'm sorry. I wish we had time for you to come to terms with all that is happening and understand, but we don't. We have life or death problems occurring, and you being vexed with Gideon or myself pales in comparison. I'm worried about you, and Gideon is sick with guilt, but I don't have time to fix this right now. He can. Please…just speak with him…for me."

Amelia growled, the sound coming out of her throat more animal than human. "Fine." She climbed off the bed, stomped past him and down the stairs without bothering to change out of the thick nightshift she wore. Downstairs she knocked one time and waited.

"What do you want, Gideon?" Amelia snapped out the instant the door to Parker's study opened.

Oddly enough her brother didn't follow her into the room, but instead he left her alone with Gideon.

"You," Gideon said simply. His face was pale compared to his usually healthy-looking features, and she could see he'd lost a bit of weight.

Parker was right—he did look sick.

"You don't really want me, whatever the mating thing is—it wants me. You're just an unfortunate host."

He smiled in sad manner. "This would be a lot easier if what you said was true."

"Isn't it?"

"Not even close. People make connections. On the rare occasion people in the *Ton* marry for love rather than titles, *that* is their connection. It's the same with creatures, it just appears differently. Most people court to develop their connection and understand they're compatible. We make the connection instantly, and the mating makes the link stronger and faster. We don't have to spend years courting to know we suit. Humans

48

develop the desire for one another, but the instant our bond is mature enough our desires are magnified—making them harder to resist. The mating doesn't make me want you, it just makes it harder for me to keep my hands off you. I do however have control over my desire. I didn't become your friend because of what we are. I just recognized your significance in my life far sooner than a normal person would have. Even if neither of us were beasts we would still suit. I would still want you, and I would still want to marry you. It probably would have taken me longer to realize it, and I might have lost you to someone else while I was figuring it out."

"Then creatures don't love?" She knew she loved him, but maybe it was because she was only half a beast. Maybe he couldn't love her because he was full-blooded. The thought made her want to retch.

"What?"

"You said normal people marry for love but with creatures it's different. Do beasts not love?"

"They love more than you can ever imagine."

"But not you."

Gideon tilted his head. "Why not me?"

"You don't love me."

A guttural sound escaped Gideon's lips. "Have you been listening to anything I have said in the last eight years?"

"You've never once said you loved me," she growled out the word. "Not once."

His eyes widened. "Is that *why*?" He took a step toward her, then stopped and began to pace. "All this time, you rejected my proposals because you thought I didn't love you?" His voice rose.

Amelia didn't answer, she couldn't. She was too close to tears.

"I don't know which is worse, the fact that you thought I would spend so much time trying to win your heart while not caring, or the fact that I assumed you would already know how I felt. I thought you just needed time, when in fact you have been waiting on me." He swore. "Of course, I love you! I have *been* in love with you. How could I not? You're the most beautiful, kind, compassionate, funny, intelligent, irresistible woman I've ever met."

Listening to his words, Amelia could feel her entire body heating with embarrassment—from the tips of her toes to the roots of her hair.

"What must you think? I attend every event you do. I enter and leave London exactly as you do. I always accept your parents' offer to dinner, and every other invitation they send! I dance with you at every ball, sit near your family at musicals and dinners. Not to mention your family is on the guest list at every function my sisters plan, and don't forget our secret rendezvous. Do you believe I'm mad to pursue you so diligently?"

"No…" She swallowed.

"You do realize that even the most enthusiastic suitors are not that dedicated, right?"

"Well, I—"

"What is it about our relationship that is not convincing to you?"

"I don't know!" She threw her hands up. "It's not unusual to me for you to be near me. You have been since we met. How was I supposed to know you did it because of me? It's not uncommon for friends to spend time together, and you are friends with my brothers too! Men take lovers all the time that they do not care for in a romantic way. How was I to know you didn't dance with me out of courtesy? Or that you sit near us because we're familiar? Or that you invite us so as not to offend us? So much of that can be explained, I'm used to you being around."

"But not everything, Amelia." Gideon lowered his voice. "Not years of making love to you in every quiet corner I can find. Not years of making sure I am there when you need me at all times. I wouldn't have told you the truth of my nature if I did not love and trust you. I would not have proposed to you nearly as many times, nor would I have pursued you for so long. I was fairly certain my affections were obvious."

"Maybe they were…maybe I was blind. I have been caught up in my own feelings for so long maybe I just didn't realize yours."

Gideon inhaled deeply in anticipation. "And what are your feelings exactly, Amelia?"

She smiled shyly. "If your feelings are so obvious, I should think mine are too. I agreed to your seductions without much hesitation. I dance with you each time you ask, and I accept every invitation your sisters send. I have never once turned you away except when I thought you'd chosen another."

"Say it. Say the words, Melia."

Gideon's beloved inhaled softly. "I have been in love with you since I was fifteen. You were the first and only man I've ever loved."

He grinned broadly. "I have dreamt of those words coming from your lips."

"Likewise," she admitted.

"Would it be too much to assume that you'll accept my proposal now," he whispered.

"Yes."

He raised one eyebrow. "I'm sorry, I thought—"

Amelia giggled. "No. I mean yes—I'll marry you."

"Truly?"

She nodded.

Gideon tugged her into his arms and held her as tightly as he dared with Parker so near, while simultaneously pressing desperate kisses into her hair. "I thought this day would never come," he admitted blissfully. *Finally,* after chasing her for so long, after making every possible attempt to convince her of his affection, Amelia had agreed to be his.

His heart nearly beat out of his chest as he held her close, basking in the devotion he felt echoing in her embrace. He'd never imagined that she'd feel as strongly for him as he did for her. As a human, he suspected she'd eventually agree to marry him out of necessity, and while it hadn't been a pleasant thought, it had at least pacified his beast.

Now he didn't have to worry about leashing his wolf. Amelia was his, and she wasn't human. She could truly understand him in a way that no mortal woman ever could, and he was beyond delighted with the turn of events.

A cough from the direction of the doorway caused Gideon and Amelia to leap away from each other.

"Parker!" Amelia all but sputtered, her cheeks red with embarrassment.

Gideon, however, grinned like a fool. He didn't care if the entire *Ton* knew she was his.

"I assume this means there will be a wedding in the

near future after all." Parker's tight smile said he would accept nothing but an affirmation.

"We can announce the engagement immediately," agreed Gideon excitedly.

"How about at your sister's event this evening? They've invited a fair number of the *Ton* from what I have heard."

"Perfect!" Gideon grinned once more. "As for that other matter, I'll be in contact soon. I need to send word to my men—they'll know more after they have scouted around."

Amelia would like to know what other matter they could possibly be discussing, especially since Parker had already mentioned he had issues that were far more important than the state of her relationship with Gideon. Clearly, her soon-to-be-husband knew what those affairs were and had put them aside to pursue their future nuptials. It appeared by Gideon's reluctance to respond outright, that neither he, nor her brother wanted her to know exactly what they were referring to. However, Amelia was tired of being kept in the dark— as she had been about her family's legacy. Had Parker truly meant it was life or death or was that his way of keeping his little sister out of dealings he felt were not any of her concern?

"I believe I hear someone at the door. Excuse me." Parker rushed out of the room, though Amelia had heard no knock.

She turned to Gideon. "Maybe I can't force my brothers to talk, but it would not be in your best interest to keep secrets from me, *mate*." She watched his pupils dilate at her use of the word, and what it meant. Her warning had the intended effect.

"How did I not notice…you have the temper of a she-wolf down perfectly."

"I'm serious, Gideon."

"As am I, my love. Do you think to threaten me?" He seemed amused.

"Oh no, darling. I think to make your life miserable." She smirked.

"How so? You have just agreed to marry me—my life is fantastic!"

She shrugged. "I suppose it depends on how soon you want me in your bed—willingly."

His grin faded. "Withholding your marital duties?" He tsked. "That's not nice."

"Neither is lying to your betrothed."

He sighed. "I can't tell you anything right now. You're still a ward of your brother, but once we're married—" He shrugged. "—I can tell you anything you want to know."

"That's ridiculous!"

"The *Ton is not the only ones who have rules*, Amelia. Shape-shifters have bylaws also. Your brother might not be able to legally keep you from me according to our laws, but you still belong to his pack until we're wed."

"You mean my family? They're considered a pack?"

"Of sorts." He nodded. "Most wolves do not live alone. We have families and friends that we consider our pack. We rely on one another. Have you never considered it odd that your brothers all remain at home, though they are old enough to have their own lodgings? Your family has plenty of money to support them all."

"Well, yes." She considered his words for a

moment. It wasn't exactly unusual for men to remain at home, but Gideon was right. Her brothers were at an age to have their own wives, homes, and children. While it was true that they could marry and move their families onto her parents' estate, she'd noticed that most men preferred their own space—especially ones who were not next in line for their family title.

Now that he'd mentioned it, however, her family was noticeably a bit strange. Other than during the season when her brothers brought her and her two younger sisters to London, they almost always did everything together. And not just her family but with Gideon's as well. It wasn't unusual at all to find both their fathers smoking a cigar in the study or to find their mothers conversing in the garden. Come to think of it, Gideon was almost always about. Even when he wasn't sneaking around with her, he was in constant talks with at least one of her brothers. To anyone else the entire relationship was probably a bit odd.

A good many of the aristocracy didn't see each other that often, and rarely did the men spend much time with their wives. The fact Gideon had made it a point to see her at least once a week since she'd met him was the strangest of all, and yet she had never truly given it much thought. Most likely because she didn't pay attention to the social rules of the *Ton,* but even so how had she not noticed?

"When you said pack, you didn't just mean your friends and family—you mean mine too and other beasts nearby, right?"

He shrugged. "I'm not sure how much your brother wants you to know, but we're all a pack in some ways, because we reside so close to each other. Your father is your alpha, with Parker next in line just like he is for the title. In my family my father has stepped down, and I lead my pack. I'm the alpha. But our families get along well, which is not exactly usual. We're lucky in that way—some packs hate each other and choose to fight over territories."

"So, all those times I talked about beasts and you brushed my interest aside, you knew they were real."

"I couldn't exactly admit the truth as long as you were turning me down. I didn't know what you were, but I talked to Parker last night and it all makes sense now. I'm sure my parents already knew, but no one thought to tell me either. I never once said you were a fool for believing in them or made you feel mad, did I?"

"Well, no," she admitted reluctantly.

"Exactly. I didn't try to convince you of anything, I let you talk about them, and I entertained your musings. I could only do so much without telling you the truth, and if you weren't going to marry me, I wouldn't be able to tell you anything at all. I didn't know you had shifter blood. I had to be careful. You could have told someone, and they would in all probability turn you over as an addlepated troublemaker, and possibly have you committed. I couldn't live with myself if that had happened."

"You would have let them commit me?"

"Of course not! I would have kidnapped you and whisked you off to Gretna Green for a quick wedding, but we would have had to abandon our families in order to protect you."

"You would have done all that for me?"

"I would do *anything* for you. You are my most beloved. My heart and soul belong to you, and they always will. I would give my life for you and give up everything I have if need be. I'm committed to you."

She promptly burst into tears. "And you couldn't have said that eight years ago? We could have been an old married couple by now!"

He chuckled and pulled her into his arms for a comforting hug. He kissed the top of her head briefly and sighed. "I'm sorry. I shouldn't have assumed anything. I was a dunce."

"Maybe," she sniffed. "But a handsome one."

He laughed then. "I'm not sure if I should accept that as a compliment or not."

"Me either," she admitted with a smile.

"I can't leave you two alone for a second," admonished Parker.

Amelia couldn't help but laugh, however, she did immediately released her beau and take a few healthy steps away from him. "I'm sorry, it was my fault."

Parker snorted. "Most things are. You're incredibly headstrong." He eyed them as he walked to his desk. "Well, now that we have this out of the way, and since it seems you will eventually be a wolf like the rest of us, I suppose I can explain a few things." He glanced at Gideon briefly and sighed. "Apparently you aren't the only one of my sisters to find her mate."

"What?" Amelia gasped and fell into one of the high wing-back chairs across from her brother's desk. "Who?"

"Lizbeth. Papa sent me a letter a couple weeks ago. It arrived today."

"But she's only fifteen."

"You were twelve when you first met Gideon," pointed out Parker dryly.

"But that's not the same thing, it wasn't *that way* then."

Gideon took the seat next to her but didn't interrupt.

Parker shrugged. "Well, Papa isn't letting hers be *that way* either. Yet. The Duke of Lunsford—who also happens to be a shifter—stopped by on his way to London with his family. It seems they were late arriving for the season due to their eldest son's wife giving birth. Anyway, the duke's youngest son, Caleb, I think his name is, apparently made a connection with Lizbeth. Now Mother and Papa are on their way here with her, so they can keep an eye on both of them."

Amelia frowned. "What does that mean exactly? Why wouldn't they just keep them apart for a few years until they're old enough?"

"Because wolves can't be away from their mates long once they've met," admitted Gideon.

Parker nodded.

"And you didn't think I should know that piece of information?" She directed a dark look in Gideon's direction.

"I told you—"

"Yes. I know. You couldn't tell me because I might tell the *Ton*." She rolled her eyes petulantly.

Gideon heaved a sigh. "I did tell you when you were fourteen. You just didn't believe me."

"Well I thought you were teasing!"

"I didn't exactly give you a reason to think I was teasing."

Amelia snorted. "You were nearly sixteen, everything you did was teasing."

He grinned.

Parker cleared his throat. "As much as I enjoy a walk down memory lane, your conversation is going to go somewhere I don't want to be, and we have more important things just now to consider. We still have three missing she-wolves and a few rogues lurking around London."

Her eyes widened, as she gawked at her brother. "What are rogues? What's a she-wolf? Am I a she-wolf?" Her head spun. Was this the matter that they had insisted was so important?

Parker shrugged. "You weren't going to be a wolf before, so you didn't need to know the truth. It would have made it harder for you to marry a human if you knew about us. Now that you're marrying a wolf, it doesn't matter if you know because it's your world too."

Amelia clamped her mouth shut. He was absolutely right. As much as it killed her to know her family had been hiding their true nature and hadn't intended to tell her, she could see the logic in his words.

"Speaking of which, you can't tell Hannah or Poppy. Our sisters are not showing any signs of being like us as far as I know. If they happen to find their mate in a wolf, we'll tell them then."

"But Parker, how can they marry human men...don't shifters age more slowly than normal people?" protested Amelia.

"Did you tell her that?" Parker demanded of Gideon.

Gideon glanced at her as if questioning whether she needed him to be her alibi.

Amelia smirked at her brother. "Considering you were going to let me marry a human without a hint of knowledge as to what I really am, I don't think I'm required to tell you."

"You're still my sister regardless, and if someone is telling you things they shouldn't be, I need to know!"

"It hardly matters now, does it?"

"Amelia, who told you?"

"Amelia, does someone else know about us?" asked Gideon softly.

"I haven't told anyone the truth—I'm not a fool. I would have been ruined, Gideon." She paused. "Why didn't I think of that before? I could have stopped coming to London *years* ago! Anyone I told would have thought my hunt for werewolves was a load of Banbury Tales, but I could've convinced them I was as mad as a hatter and gone home."

"Amelia!" Parker groused. "Just tell me where you got the information."

"I do have other friends, Parker. And not all of them brushed aside my anecdotes of shape-shifters the way you did. Some of them entertained my notions and enjoyed pondering their existence with me."

"I have only seen you talking to Gideon and…the Duke of Covington's daughter!" He gasped and looked at Gideon. "It was Beatrix. Are they shifters?"

Gideon nodded. "Full-blooded."

"Fiend seize it to hell! She's telling people?" Parker rose. "I have to deal with this. I'm leaving you here to watch over my sister, and I swear if you don't keep your hands off her…" He raised a clenched fist in emphasis.

"It's a little late for that speech."

Parker gnashed his teeth at Gideon's response and rushed out the door without another word.

Amelia wasn't sure what would happen to her friend, but then it wasn't as if she'd betrayed her intentionally either. She couldn't very well name a random girl she'd never even spoken to. Beatrix had also mentioned she *believed* wolves could sense a lie. Not that Amelia made a habit of lying, but it was good to know anyway. It also explained why she could sense when people weren't being honest with her. Apparently, Beatrix's *theories* held some truth after all. She wondered if her friend had admitted the truth in jest, or if she'd intentionally been trying to enlighten Amelia to the fact of the matter without admitting it outright.

Gideon grinned. "All this time I have been one of your closest confidants aside from Beatrix, and you didn't consider that unusual when you were wondering what my intentions were?"

Amelia didn't know what to say, so she shrugged her shoulders.

His grin widened. "I've been your neighbor, lover, and best friend…any other roles I might play in your life?"

"Husband."

Gideon leaned over the edge of his chair toward her. "Keep that up, and Parker will have to draw my cork again when he gets back, because I'm not going to be able to keep from touching you."

"Speaking of Parker, what is he doing?"

"Since he's deemed you're to know everything and I obviously want you to as well, London is neutral territory. Everyone except rogues are allowed in the city. We all have a set of codes we have to abide by, and if something unique occurs that doesn't fit in our rules, every alpha in the city meets in a secret location to vote on the matter. Typically, we're able to handle things ourselves. Parker, as your acting alpha since your father isn't here—his job is to protect you and your siblings. If someone told you about shifter secrets while believing you were a human, then they inadvertently put you in danger, and it's his duty to handle the indiscretion."

"How is he going to *handle* it?" demanded Amelia suspiciously.

"Beatrix might have been irresponsible, but she could have done worse. Most likely he'll confront her father, and her father will deal with her. Since she's a female, it's her alpha's responsibility to protect her, and Parker is technically a threat."

"How is he a threat? He isn't going to attack her, surely?"

"All males are considered a threat to females. We're usually stronger and faster than you, even if you were in wolf form. It's our duty to protect our females, so it makes sense that anyone outside your pack would be a threat. Her father will see that Parker doesn't mean Beatrix any harm though. Don't worry. It's just shifter politics."

"Much like ridiculous society rules," she groaned. "And here I thought I had almost outgrown those."

Gideon laughed out loud. "Have no fear, my beloved. When we're married you may enter society as little as you wish. We can stay home in the country as much as you want."

Amelia grinned. "I hadn't considered you would feel that way. Perhaps I *should* have married you in order to escape the *Ton*."

Gideon gasped in feigned betrayal. He clutched a hand over his heart dramatically and whined. "You wound me. And here I thought you were true in your devotion! Had I known you accepted my proposal simply to put society behind you, I might have reconsidered!"

"I'm sure my willingness to warm your bed would distract you from my ulterior motives sufficiently."

His eyes darkened at her words, and he leaned in closer. "The odds of me getting you alone before our wedding, now that your brothers know about us, are nonexistent. Don't tempt the beast, Melia. I only have so much control over him, and you are much too delicious to resist."

Amelia shivered at his words.

"Even when you don't mean to react, I'm still lured by your responses."

She considered her options. She could appear the meek miss and put him off her scent, or she could embrace this dangerous version of her future husband and see how far she could push him. Amelia grinned mischievously. "You know, thus far our meetings have been rather rushed. I can only imagine how much fun they'll be after we're married and have no restraints."

He growled low, an unnatural animalistic warning sound that had Amelia's insides stirring to life.

Something shifted within her, and she marveled at the new sensation.

"I imagine I can learn a great deal of things when I have nothing better to do than seduce my *mate*."

"Amelia," he warned again, his voice low and raspy.

Her insides shifted once more, and a flood of

euphoria washed over her as she felt something lurking inside of her—twisting seductively. Whatever this new feeling was, it felt alive and seemed to have its own thoughts and opinions. It agreed with Amelia's emotions and seemed to mirror the effects of Gideon's growl on her body. It felt dark and dangerous—like a separate entity from herself, and yet it felt like a part of her too. It was protective, and it *loved* Gideon's attention. This new being associated with Amelia as if they were of one mind like her subconscious, but stronger, and it moved through her as if they shared one body.

Amelia sat back in the chair, her focus on the new sensation rather than Gideon.

"What's wrong?" he asked, his voice filled with concern. "You look sick. You're not—"

He didn't finish the sentence, but Amelia knew what he meant.

"No. I have had my flow since the last time we were together." She felt her rib cage. "I feel strange."

"Strange how?"

She touched her stomach experimentally, and though she didn't feel anything unusual she did sense something different—female and primal. It insisted she touch Gideon, and in an effort to appease the demands, Amelia touched his arm experimentally.

He watched her with some obvious confusion but didn't hesitate to take her hand in his. "Maybe you should lie down?"

"She likes it when I touch you."

"*She*? Are you telling me you can feel your wolf? Amelia, that's impossible. I haven't marked you."

"I don't know *what* it is," growled Amelia in

frustration. "It just feels like there's something inside me, and it's talking to me—sort of. Not exactly with words, but I feel its thoughts or maybe its emotions, and when you growled at me it felt…" She frowned. "I think it *liked* it."

"Amelia."

She ignored him. "I'm not crazy, Gideon. It wants me to taunt you. She likes when you hunt me." Amelia hesitated. "I don't even know what that means."

"I technically hunt you every day. Any time I show up in the same location as you, simply because you're there, I'm pursuing you. But you wouldn't realize that unless you were full-blooded. Again, I haven't marked you, and you shouldn't be able to feel her until I do."

"I have too many clothes on," gasped Amelia suddenly as her entire body began to burn.

"Amelia, no, breathe through it."

"Through *what*?"

"She wants you to shift. Ignore her. It's just because your skin feels too tight, but you don't need to be naked to shift, your clothes will melt away as you change. She can't control you, Melia, she *is* you. Just take deep breaths and focus on me."

"But it's too hot in here," she whined.

"That's what the change feels like, but you don't have to shift. You can ignore your inner wolf. Look at me. Focus, breathe."

Amelia forced her attention back to Gideon. Handsome, funny, intelligent, Gideon. Her fiancé and *mate*. Her body began to ache, and she clenched her jaw in response to the growing tenderness of her flesh. She stared into his eyes in an effort to leash her more primal desires, and while her body seemed to calm under his influence, something else stirred. She wanted him to touch her, and she didn't care if he knew.

"Gideon." She dragged in a deep breath.

"Your brother will be back soon," he implored.

"But I can't—" She bit her lip anxiously. "—I need—" She forced her mouth to close on the words.

"I know, my love, I know. There's no way this should be happening. I'm so sorry. I should have kept my hands to myself, but when you look at me like that—" He swallowed.

"I can't help it," she complained softly. "I want you. Before it was just a craving, but now I feel as if my body will go up in flames if I don't touch you."

Gideon dropped to his knees before her and took her hands in his palms. He leaned forward and pressed his lips against her forehead. "It's all right, Melia, you don't need to feel that way. I'm yours. I swear it— always."

"What did you mean when you said you hadn't marked me?"

"After we're married, I can claim you. I'll bite you, and it'll act as a mating mark. You'll bear my scent just as you'll bear my last name, and other males will know that you're mine."

"And what about the females?" She all but snarled as a burst of jealousy rushed through her.

He chuckled. "You can claim me too—it works the same way."

She was momentarily pacified, but it didn't last long. "But I haven't claimed you. You're a duke, Gideon. Any other woman would have said yes to you, if you had asked for their hand."

"But I don't want anyone else. Only you,

remember? You have me—you have since we met—you just didn't know. You have to tell your inner wolf to stop worrying, she's magnifying your insecurities. I belong with you. She doesn't understand our ways. She only understands the need to mate. You have to keep her under control, otherwise the *Ton* will find out about us and we'll be hunted."

"Tare an' hounds, Gideon! I specifically asked you to keep your hands off my sister," roared Parker from the doorway, interrupting their hushed conversation, yet again. "I have enough to deal with as it is. I don't need to be constantly worried about you two!"

Gideon didn't move away from her. "Not now, Parker."

When her brother stomped across the floor toward them, she tried to tell her inner beast to back down and it seemed to work, but when Parker began to curse again, the creature wanted to assert her own dominance and inflict *her* will on Parker. The emotion was a nearly irresistible urge to bring Parker under control, as if she could somehow force her brother to submit to her demands as easily as he'd gotten her to submit to his while being her guardian.

"You marked her! Have you gone insane?" exclaimed Parker.

"No," growled Gideon. "I didn't. I swear. I seduced her—I admitted as much, but I never bit her."

Parker swore. "She can't be shifting without your bite, Gideon."

"Maybe it's because I'm an alpha, her wolf is stronger than it should be. She's an alpha's mate so her wolf has to be an alpha too. Maybe that's why Amelia can unleash her without the bite?"

Parker groaned. "I don't know! I'm a half-blood, remember? I don't know as much as you do."

"I don't exactly keep up with the wolf dating traditions, and this isn't something I've ever encountered," admitted Gideon.

Amelia pushed out of Gideon's arms and stood. She took a threatening step toward her brother—who was standing on the opposite side of the desk, but she paused in an effort to gain control. She placed her hands on the edge of the wooden surface, lowered her head, and held her breath against the fire that rushed renewed throughout her body—incinerating her from the inside out. The beast had long since settled and seemed to be just as concerned about the flames licking along her body as was Amelia.

"I'm her alpha. I can order her to stop, can't I?" insisted Parker.

Gideon shrugged. "In theory."

"Amelia, don't change!"

She heard her brother's command and felt something push at her that was akin to an invisible hand attempting to force her compliance, but she ignored the compulsion. She suddenly felt powerful and unrestrained, and she wondered if this was what a young child felt like the first time it learned to walk. She was both amazed and terrified by her newly discovered strength. Her fists clenched, and she felt the wood of the desk crack under the pressure. Her fingers ached and felt warm and wet, but she kept her eyes closed. She focused her attention on forcing the desire to override her brother's authority back under control.

"Amelia, I command you to stop!" Parker tried again with more authority in his voice.

She felt the same push try to assert itself once more, but it seemed to roll right off her as if it hadn't even touched her.

"Melia, you have to stop your wolf," added Gideon gently.

Both of them were giving her an order, but she didn't feel inclined to listen, nor to explain that it wasn't her wolf, but a mutual desire they shared to assert her dominance that now tried to control her.

"That should have worked," growled Parker.

"She should have responded to one of us at least," agreed Gideon in confusion.

"I don't understand." Her brother sounded disconcerted.

"When you tell me to stop…. I feel it like a whisper, but she says I don't have to listen, that I don't have to do what you say. She says we're free of your command. What does that even mean?" breathed out Amelia desperately.

Gideon swore. "It means you're not an alpha, beta, *or* submissive."

"She's an Omega?" asked Parker.

Gideon sighed. "Does your father know?"

"How could he? She's never shifted before."

Amelia shook her head in annoyance. Sweat beaded her brow, and her entire body was wet with perspiration. The heat began to subside slowly, but she still felt it tugging at her, demanding control.

Gideon's hand rested on her back now, rubbing in long slow circles up and down Amelia's spine, offering the only comfort he could in front of her brother.

She wanted to tell her brother to go away, that she didn't need him to tell her what to do, but the normal part of her knew it wasn't his fault. It wasn't anyone's fault.

"If Amelia's an Omega, there's a good chance your other sisters are too. They can't marry human men, Parker—they might shift without the mark. You have to tell your father."

"He'll make them go back to the country. He'll never let them in society again. How will they find their mates out there?"

"They could change in *public*, Parker!" Gideon's voice belied the horror behind his words.

"I know!" her brother shouted back.

Amelia's beast didn't like Gideon mentioning her sisters, but she reined the creature under control. Gideon was *hers*, and her sisters were not her competition. They were not a threat to her. She had to remind herself of this fact repeatedly until the fever finally subsided, and she was left a panting mess.

Finally, after moments of forced relaxation she released the edge of the desk and opened her eyes. Blood coated her hands, and she gasped at the sight of claw marks embedded where she'd grasped the wood.

"You partially shifted," explained Gideon as if he sensed her anxiety. He continued to rub her back and seemed to want to do more, but Parker still stood there as well. "You did beautifully while bringing her under control. I'm proud of you."

"Those are claw marks." Amelia was aghast.

"It's normal for us."

"That's not normal!"

"I've ruined plenty of furniture, Amelia," admitted Parker reluctantly. "Don't you remember that table in the entry that mysteriously disappeared the night I was caught sneaking a smoke?"

"You don't smoke," she argued.

Parker smirked. "Not anymore." He reached into his breast pocket and removed a thin white handkerchief and offered it to her without explanation.

"Someone will notice," whispered Amelia shakily, while scrubbing the blood from her palms. Already her torn skin had closed up, which was amazing in itself.

Gideon leaned forward, placed both of his hands on the lip of the desk, and shoved it down hard toward the floor. The wood splintered and snapped away, and he tossed it into the fireplace. "Now it just looks like Parker had a fit." He grinned.

Parker grunted. "That's honestly more believable anyway. I have news. Normally I would wait for our brothers, but this concerns you too, Amelia, since she's your friend, and I've finally had the chance to make her acquaintance." Parker's change of subject released her from the guilt of having destroyed his desk.

"What did you do to Beatrix?" accused Amelia.

"Nothing." Parker raised his hands defensively. "I met her."

"And?"

"And…I understand now…why Gideon couldn't leave you alone."

"You poor bastard." Gideon followed his words with a grin.

"I don't understand."

"Beatrix is your brother's mate, Amelia."

"You must've seen me with her before. I talk to her at nearly every event she bothers to attend. You didn't sense her relevance to you before now?" asked Amelia in confusion.

Parker sighed. "Honestly, Amelia, if it wasn't an undesirable male approaching you, I didn't feel like I needed to intervene. You have to understand, there are so many scents and people at these blasted events it's hard to differentiate one from the other. And she hasn't ever called on you here—not when I was in, and I'd never gotten a decent whiff of her before now. Had I known what she was whispering in your ear, however…"

"Why do you feel sorry for him? You seemed to think our mating was the greatest thing to ever happen," demanded Amelia, her attention shifting from her brother to her mate.

"Oh, it is…for me. I could remain close to you. I have…er…" He cleared his throat. "I have been *lucky*. It's not as easy when it's the other way around. Beatrix is full-blooded, and her father doesn't have to consent because Parker is halfblooded."

"But Parker is going to be a duke."

"We're considered mutts in their world," clarified Parker.

Amelia gaped at Gideon as if it was his fault. "Excuse me?"

"Not to me!" Gideon glared at her brother. "Why the hell did you tell her that?"

"It's true. If she had been full-blood and you the half-blood, you know as well as I that it would have been damn hard to convince our father that you're worthy of her."

Gideon sighed. "That's true, but—"

"So now I'm not worthy?" She crossed her arms angrily, overwhelmed by these new and intense feelings racing through her body, making her an emotional wreck. "I was clearly worthy when you took my virginity in the garden when I was only eighteen." She shoved Gideon away from her and stormed out of her brother's study.

"Amelia," objected Gideon. "I never said you weren't worthy!" He heaved a sigh of frustration and followed her out into the hall, where she spun back toward him—her eyes glittering furiously. He'd only just convinced her to marry him, and already he was on the verge of losing her once more. He searched for a way to console her rage, but she wasn't to be contained. Her wolf would not allow her to be reasonable. She was overwhelmed, and her body nearly hummed with anger. But there was nothing he could do, no relief he could offer other than to let her vent her frustrations—at least not with her brother around. There was plenty he could do in private to calm her wolf, but he had to concede to the rules of society in that moment. Parker would accept nothing less.

"No wonder your cousin suggested that half-wit for you. Apparently, I am a lesser being and don't *deserve* someone so *grand* as yourself." She bowed sarcastically as if he were a prince. "How dare I fall in love with a *Full-Blood* when I'm merely a *mutt*!"

"Ironically, that's technically a step up from when he thought you were human," chirped Parker loudly from the other room.

"Parker," bellowed Gideon.

"Right! You knew I wasn't good enough from the beginning, and yet you still made me think I had a chance. You treated me as if I mattered. Was this all a sick game to you? Did you think me nothing but a light skirt that you could play with until a *real* shifter came

73

along?" She didn't stop to listen but continued toward the entry where the stairs to her room would provide her with the dramatic exit she craved.

"Amelia! I have never thought of you that way—only as my lover and beloved. Are you even hearing yourself? I wouldn't give a damn if you didn't have a single drop of shifter blood in your entire body. Hell, you could be a lady's maid, and I would still marry you today. My family—other than my parents and siblings—don't even know your name. They have no idea that I have already met my mate, but if they had Tristan would have never suggested *any* other female. It doesn't matter to anyone, especially not me or my family who you are." He followed after her, trying in vain to make her understand.

Gideon wasn't a bit surprised by Amelia's histrionic reaction. His childhood experiences with her advised him to expect nothing short of a full-blown temper tantrum. He wouldn't normally be worried, except that even during her most dramatic moments, Amelia always seemed to at least hear his protests. He knew she prided herself on being a logical thinker, but he also knew his mate was passionate about the things that mattered to her, and this most definitely mattered. Hell—it mattered to him! He couldn't have his mate thinking she was less than he was, or that she didn't deserve his love. He needed her to be as confident about their relationship as he was, because the moment she stopped believing in herself, was the moment he'd lose her for good. He couldn't let that happen. He couldn't ever let her think less of herself. It was his responsibility as her mate to always build her up, *never* to tear her down.

Gideon realized Amelia didn't want to believe him, and even though she didn't stop to hear his objections, he knew that as a wolf she heard every uttered word just fine. She did, *however,* immediately freeze in the entryway when she realized they weren't alone.

Not only was Hadley standing there silently, hearing it all, but so were Gideon's parents.

Gideon's mother smiled warmly. "Little one, you needn't worry, we love you just as you are."

Amelia so wanted to cry. Her entire body ached, and her mind divided between wanting to kiss and kill Gideon. Her heart stung with the pain of betrayal, and now she was thoroughly humiliated. In that moment she would have given anything to have her mother there to hold her and promise everything would be all right. It didn't matter she was no longer a child—she'd always been close with her parents. She also had a warm relationship with Gideon's parents. If she was honest, they had been like a second mother and father to her while growing up. She didn't need to put up a front with them. They'd seen her rolling in the mud with their son after he'd broken her favorite doll.

For a moment she stood there debating on her next move, and then Gideon's mother lifted her arms to offer a hug, and it was as if the entire world came crashing down on Amelia's shoulders. She practically leapt into the woman's arms, and every tear she'd been holding back came rushing out in great ugly sobs.

"There, there, now, dearest. Come with me." Amelia didn't know where they were going, and she didn't care. "Go away, Gideon. This is women's business," his mother admonished.

Seeing her fiancé shooed away like a naughty

schoolboy almost made Amelia laugh. Gideon had always been older, taller, stronger, and quicker, but his mother had reduced him to an unruly child. It felt good to feel as if the woman was on her side.

"I'll be in the study with Parker if you need me," muttered Gideon.

Amelia didn't respond.

His mother led her farther down the hall and into the drawing room. After she closed the door behind them, she walked Amelia to a long settee.

Amelia continued to sniff tearfully, but her sobs had subsided.

"Tell me, little one, what has my son done to you?"

"He didn't do anything."

"Well what *hasn't* he done, then?"

"He's *perfect*."

"Come now, he's my son. Remember? I know him too well. You can tell me."

"He loves me, and apparently he always has."

"Well…yes."

Amelia sniffed again. "But he's a full-blooded shifter, and I didn't even know I was a half-blooded one."

"All right."

"And apparently that means I'm a mutt, and I'm not good enough for him."

"Did he say that?"

"No."

"Oh, good. I feared I might have to put him over my knee," Gideon's mother admitted with a soft chuckle.

"But I didn't know any of this." Amelia swiped at the remainder of her tears. "How was I supposed to know he was serious when he proposed all those other times?"

"It's all right, dear. There is nothing for you to be ashamed of. You are a beautiful, smart, young woman. My son is lucky to have found you. I know you will make a lovely bride. You have never been anything less than you are, and you are perfect for Gideon in every way."

"I'm a mutt."

"You hush now. It doesn't make one bit of difference to anyone who cares. No one else matters. Our family loves you, and my son loves you. I will be honored to have you as my daughter-in-law. You are already a daughter in my heart, regardless."

"Honestly?"

"Yes. I look forward to the day when you and Gideon are wed!"

Amelia managed a soft smile. "I accepted his proposal."

"I'm so glad. Just don't let him boss you around," teased the older woman.

"He can't, I'm an Omega. Whatever *that* is."

Mrs. Rochester grinned. "It means you are unique and rare and even more wonderful than you already were."

"Can I ask you a question?"

"Of course."

"Does Gideon like me because I'm his mate, or am I his mate because he likes me?"

"It's a little of both I believe. It's complicated. The ancients believed that a human body was not strong enough to house an entire soul. So, they split it into two parts and sent both off into the world. Should the two halves be lucky enough to reunite they would become whole again. You are Gideon's mate—therefore you are the other half of his soul, and vice versa he is the other part of yours. You are one when you are together. This occurs in humans too, but they do not have the same instinct. As wolves we can sense when we have found our other half. That's why we call them a mate. It means you are destined. Simply put, you and my son belong together. He has known it for many years, and we made a great effort to get to know your family because he needed you in his life—even though he thought you to be human. We have come to love your entire family as if you were part of our own pack. I have watched over you as if you were my own blood at times, and as long as I have known you, I can honestly say that I could not ask for a better wife for my son."

"Then you don't think I'm unworthy because I'm not a full-blood?"

Gideon's mother laughed. "No, little one. Our family has never cared for nonsensical politics. Many of our kind don't. We do not choose who we love, so why should it matter to anyone else? Gideon loves you, and that's all that matters."

"If you're here I can only imagine that my own parents are on their way."

"Due to arrive within the hour," Gideon's mother confirmed.

Amelia groaned. "I suppose I should sort this out with Gideon before they arrive."

The duchess smiled and kissed her on the forehead. "That's a good idea." She stood and left the room, leaving Amelia to her thoughts.

Never once in her entire life had Amelia felt

unwanted, but the instant her brother said the word mutt, her entire world had shifted. Parker was a duke's first born, and he would inherit the title. He had as much money as anyone in the *Ton*, a good reputation, and would make any woman a good husband. He was kind, and he didn't drink. Any of the *Ton's* ladies would accept him, but because their mother was human he could lose his destined mate. It seemed so unfair! Beatrix was her friend, and she wasn't the type of girl to snub someone, let alone a future duke, even if he was a mutt. But Beatrix's father? Amelia didn't know him well enough to say, but she hoped he wouldn't be too quick to judge her family.

"Amelia?" Gideon stood cautiously in the doorway as if he wasn't sure if he should enter.

"I won't bite," she teased, then instantly regretted her choice of words. "I guess that's not entirely true," she muttered.

"There are too many people in this house for me to respond to your words the way I would if we were alone." He took a few steps into the room and hesitated. "I hope you don't honestly believe anything you said earlier."

She sighed. "I don't know what I believe anymore."

"I thought you were fine with me being a shifter."

"I'm perfectly fine with *you* being a shifter. It's a different game when I am too. All my life I have been the eldest daughter of a duke, nothing more, nothing less. I was expected to make a good match and produce lots of little heirs, and that was all. I was supposed to keep my mouth shut and do what society told me. But I didn't. I didn't do any of what was required. Now there are all these other rules and expectations, and they're even more overwhelming than the others."

"One second—you're not upset because you might turn into a wolf, you're upset because there are new rules to follow?" He chuckled. "You're incredible! Of all the things to be concerned about, those are the *least* of your worries. Our rules are easy compared to society's decorum. Trust me, you have nothing to worry about."

"As a woman of the *Ton*, I am expected to keep my opinion to myself, guard my virtue, and follow orders. I'm required to go to whatever social event my brother decrees necessary, and to stand prettily in the corner and wait for some poor man to ask me to dance. But only once because people might assume we're engaged otherwise. Then I'm supposed to come home and sleep in my own bed, *alone*, and wait for my brother *or father* to announce where I must go next—every day, until some wealthy titled man asks me to be his wife. Then I must live with him, perform wifely duties, and do whatever *he* says for the rest of my life. I was almost free of all that. A few more years and the majority of the *London's aristocracy* would have considered me on the shelf for certain.

"Now I'm mated, a wolf, and there are *new* rules to follow to go with all the others. I have to control this burning desire to rip my clothes off, and I'm forced to keep my hands off you despite the fact every part of my body is screaming at me to touch you. I apparently break furniture with my bare hands now, and I have an insatiable urge to rip apart any female that might stand too close to you. This is insane! I am not a violent person! When I thought I was human, I didn't care if you could sprout fangs and fur. I was perfectly content becoming your wife, because I knew you wouldn't make me go through this ridiculous society nonsense. I didn't know you felt like this *all the time*! I have only been this way for an hour, but you've been doing it your whole life." She was nearly in tears again as she covered her eyes with her palms.

"I'm sorry. I'm so sorry I didn't take you seriously. I'm sorry that you had to go through this. I'm sorry I made you feel like this. I'm sorry for every man I ever danced with that wasn't you and every time I said no when you asked me to marry you. I'm sorry—"

"Stop, Amelia."

She felt his arms around her shoulders, and he pulled her close to his chest.

"You don't have to do this. You don't owe me anything."

"For years you pretended like it was enough, that it didn't bother you if I danced with someone else no matter how innocent. You hid it all so well. The instant it hit me I fall apart like a ninny."

He chuckled, and she felt him kiss the top of her head.

"You're brave, Amelia. So brave. You've known for only a week that I'm not normal, and yet you're not afraid of me. You still wanted to be with me. You're not the least bit concerned that you're going to change into a wolf. Your biggest fear is breaking a rule. Don't you see how amazing that is? I was terrified of telling you about my heritage. For so long I have been trying to figure out how to tell you in a way that wouldn't traumatize you. I was so afraid of losing you. You have no idea how scared I was last week when you insinuated we were over. I don't want to exist without you, and if that means returning to the country the instant we're married and never stepping foot off the property ever again, then I'll be the happiest damn recluse that ever lived. I love you, and I'll do anything you want."

"Teach me," whispered Amelia softly. "Teach me how to be a wolf like you."

His grip tightened. "Absolutely."

****

Gideon held his mate tightly, the scent of her body like a drug—calming his inner beast. She didn't have a traditional scent like most shape-shifters, which was alarming, to say the least, but her personal scent called to him and urged him to take her in his arms and solve all her problems, as if he alone could save her. He was one man, an alpha no less, but he knew he'd try. He'd rather die than see her hurt.

The fact that she'd been about to shift, even without his bite, was terrifying. If all half-blooded females could shift without being activated, the entire world would know they existed in a matter of days. Half-blooded females were not traditionally taught the ways of shifters, because most of them never met their mates. It was unkind to introduce them to a world where others would not accept them. Without an alpha, they had nothing to tie them to a pack. They needed a mate to shift and be able to protect themselves in a world where weaker beings typically didn't survive.

Amelia was by no means weak, but he didn't blame her family for wanting to protect her against the harsh realities of being a shape-shifter. Their society was not for the faint of heart. He knew his mate would do well—he had confidence in her—but he could only imagine what might have happened if she'd gone into the world believing herself to be a human, and then accidentally shifted in front of humans. She would have been killed. His heart thumped painfully at the thought, and he held her a little tighter wanting to protect her from the world.

Soon enough he'd make sure she knew everything she needed to know to survive.

Aside from making certain Amelia was ready for their world and vice versa, she was also easy pickings for the rogues polluting his territory. It was bad enough that he was losing females left and right, despite the fact he was doing everything in his power to find them, but those were full-blooded females that *knew* and had been trained in the world of shape-shifters. He could only imagine what would happen if one was to come across Amelia, and he'd be damned if he let it happen.

Chapter Six

Amelia stood on the edge of the dance floor between Gideon's twin sisters—hiding from her own parents. She had not yet seen them since their arrival in London, as they'd needed to make sure Amelia's younger sister experienced no ill effects during travel away from her soon-to-be mate.

She knew the instant they found her that her father would be able to scent Gideon on her person. The man had held and kissed her far too many times recently for a full-blooded shifter not to notice. She was lucky no one had spoken to them about Amelia's own troubles, and both were far too concerned with Parker and his newly-found mate for the moment. Thankfully. She could see and watch them from the corner where she'd secluded herself, and her heart raced.

Gideon hadn't found her yet either, though she suspected it wouldn't take him long once he did set out to do so. Thus far he had been deluged by guests, and she was grateful for a chance to avoid him as well. Not that she wanted to evade him, not entirely or for long, but as soon as he got close to her she'd want to touch him, and they would most definitely be caught. Her parents were going to come looking for her eventually, and she did not under any circumstances want them to find her with her skirt up around her hips.

Instead she'd stolen behind an overly large potted

plant—her emerald gown blending perfectly with the foliage, while Gideon's beautiful sisters stood guard. She'd always been particularly fond of them and had on occasion been friendly, but Gideon had always been her partner. Yet, now that they knew she was Gideon's intended, and Amelia knew they were wolves, his siblings were infinitely friendlier. Apparently, it had been hard for them to keep the secret, and now his siblings were all too willing to help her hide from everyone, including their brother.

Amelia would have rather been anywhere but in Gideon's ballroom, with her parents, siblings, and the *Ton* gathered around them. She would have happily stuck pins in her arm if it meant she could go home, but it seemed she was to suffer. Thankfully no one had noticed her yet, or at least she hoped not.

"You know, that ficus is lovely, but it doesn't do you justice."

Amelia spun around in surprise to face Gideon's mother. She was alone, thankfully.

"Oh…I was just…"

"Hiding? Yes, I'm aware. I hid in that very spot thirty years ago when my own engagement was to be announced in this same ballroom."

Amelia felt her face heat. "It's not that I don't want to marry Gideon."

"I know, dearest. But your parents will understand. I have it on good authority that your mother wasn't an innocent miss on her wedding day either, and I most certainly wasn't."

"I never said—"

"You don't have to." She tapped the side of her nose and winked. "I know my son, and I know he's been in love with you for quite some time. It was bound to happen sooner or later. Though from what I can tell it was sooner."

"I was weak… I didn't even hesitate," admitted Amelia with a groan.

"It happens to the best of us. The males tend to be incredibly charming." She smiled. "Besides, I heard a rumor that your eldest brother only assaulted him twice. I doubt your father will do much more."

"It's not Gideon's fault."

"He knew what he was doing, dear one, so he obviously thought you were worth whatever punishment he would have to face." Her eyes sparkled with amusement. "I believe those are your parents coming this way now," the duchess announced before stepping back to mingle with the ball attendees.

Amelia inhaled and held her breath, rallying her courage as they appeared at her side.

Her mother smiled lovingly and hugged her. In turn her father smiled, sniffed, and immediately grumbled unintelligibly beneath his breath as he too hugged her.

"At least tell me you agreed to marry him this time," he huffed in annoyance.

Amelia swallowed once and nodded.

He sighed. "There's that at least."

"Don't tell me…" murmured Amelia's mother. At her father's nod, her mother continued. "I was wondering how long this would go on."

"You *knew*?"

"I knew he was like your father, and I knew he was in love with you. He offered to be your partner when we hired the dance tutor to teach you a proper waltz. No boy his age would have been interested in having his toes stepped on all day if he wasn't interested in the girl doing the stepping," explained Amelia's mother with an empathetic smile.

Her father coughed and looked away.

"As I said," continued her mother, "people in love do strange things. Will you be announcing your engagement this evening or allow us to do so?"

Amelia nodded. "Gideon wants to do the honor. And just so you know, Parker has already hit him twice…please let that be enough," she pleaded with her father.

Her father glanced sideways toward the guests converging in the ball room. "He's lucky that's all he got."

Her mother smacked his arm playfully. "I seem to recall someone else breaking rules as well, and my father letting *him* off easy."

"Yes, well, your father was human. All he cared about was that I was titled, rich, and not going to abuse you."

"I love him," admitted Amelia softly.

"Of course you do," whispered her mother. "You wouldn't have tolerated everything he did to you growing up. He may have been sweet to you, but he's still a boy none the less, and they are the most frustrating creatures."

Amelia heard Gideon's mother laugh as well when she rejoined them.

"I noticed Gideon is still alive."

Amelia's father muttered something beneath his breath once more, and both women chuckled.

"It appears my son isn't the only alpha you have wrapped around your finger." Gideon's mother smiled kindly. Her gaze moved from Amelia's. "I see my husband attempting to escape into the study. Excuse me."

"Actually, I need to have a word with him," groused Amelia's father, and he followed Gideon's mother.

Amelia's mother laughed softly. "I had better go make sure he doesn't change his mind and decide to kill your betrothed."

Finally, Amelia was blessedly alone. Her anxiety was at an all-time high, and she was about to experience something she'd never would have considered possible—the vapors. She noticed Gideon heading toward her and decided it was as good a time as ever to make an escape before someone spotted them alone together.

Moments later she was standing on a balcony at the end of the hall directly off the ballroom taking in the fresh night air as if she might never breathe again.

"I think they planned to ambush you that way, and I believed my mother was rescuing you from your parents, when I spotted her making her way toward you. Now, I feel she was simply stalling to give them a chance to catch up," interjected a soft male voice.

Amelia heaved a throaty sigh. It was so nice to hear his voice. She turned to face him and melted in relief when a light breeze wafted through her pinned up tresses. "I'm *dying*."

"You look beautiful. I'm the one who's about to die. I saw your father. He's going to murder me."

"I bought you some time. If you run, you might make it to Scotland before he finds you."

"That wouldn't stop him. You're his daughter. He

would do anything for you." Gideon smiled. "Just as I would. He loves you."

"He's speaking with your father now."

Gideon nodded. "No doubt they're discussing your transition into our pack."

"Shouldn't you be party to that conversation? You are an alpha."

He shrugged. "I'd rather be out here with you."

"That's what got us into this mess."

Gideon laughed out loud. "Tonight, I'm not concerned about anything but you. I can worry about everything else tomorrow."

"Everything else? What's happened?"

"Another girl went missing—this one was a friend of my sisters. The rogues are becoming dangerously bolder. But let's not worry about that right now. I have plenty of men out searching for them, and they'll report back if they find anything important. Your brother has a number of people out looking as well, and I have it on good authority that a few other alphas have their own men out as well. There's little else we can do right now. I just want to focus on you."

Amelia frowned. "But this announcement is just a formality from what I understand. It's more important to find those poor girls."

"You're right, but the addition of a new pack member is pretty important as well. Especially when it's an alpha's mate and an Omega no less."

"I'd marry you tonight and be done with it if it means you can divert more energy into the hunt."

He grinned. "Spoken like a true alpha."

"I'm an Omega, remember?"

"Precisely. You are perfect."

Amelia sighed. "This is probably the most difficult thing I have ever had to do."

"Face the *Ton*?"

"Keep my hands off of you."

"It won't be much longer, and I'll have you all to myself," Gideon promised

"Our wedding isn't for weeks."

He smirked. "There isn't a prayer in hell of me staying away from you that long. As much as they'd prefer to think otherwise, they know we're going to figure out a way—they went through it too. It's inevitable. In fact—" He glanced back over his shoulder, and then reached through the door to close the curtains and the French doors as well, shielding them from the rest of the *attendees*.

"Now I have a moment to appreciate the cut of your dress." He inched forward, grabbed her hand, and led Amelia toward the side of the balcony, where the terrace and a column didn't quite meet, creating a small nook. "They won't spot us even if they look out the window," Gideon assured her in a whisper. Amelia's heart beat so hard, it fairly leapt from her chest. It was true she'd made love with him regularly, but never in his own home, and not after learning her true nature. It was as if she were an innocent again, and she had no idea what was about to happen.

"I've missed you," he whispered, and pulled her into his arms. "I haven't gone this long without touching you in years."

"It's only been two weeks," she teased.

"I know!" He pouted dramatically. "It feels like forever."

"You realize if my father finds us, I won't be able

to save you this time?"

He shrugged. "I'll die happy." His hands slid down her bodice, and he pulled her tighter against him.

Amelia lifted her hands to his chest and melted against him. The need to feel his skin against hers was far greater than her will to survive her father's wrath.

"I'm sure I don't need to say this," she began as he kissed her throat. "But after we're married this will happen much more often, right? It isn't just the risk of getting caught that appeals to you?"

"Dearest Melia, you have no idea the beast I'll unleash once we're married. This is but a taste of what's to come. Soon there will be no barriers, and I will devour you in ways you've only dreamt of."

She giggled as his lips continued to assault the column of her throat. "You have no idea the things I have fantasized about with you."

"I look forward to making each and every one of your fantasies come true, my beloved."

One hand slid up the front of her bodice as she arched into him, stopping only when he reached her breasts.

"I want so badly to strip you bare and taste every inch of your delectable flesh. Due to the circumstances of trying not to get caught, I've only seen you completely naked once, and it's taunted me for years."

When Gideon's tongue darted out to taste the top of her bare shoulder, Amelia whimpered and bit her lip in an effort to extinguish any other sounds.

"After we're married, I'll bite you here." He suckled lightly on her collar bone—teasing her skin. "And though the mark will fade, my scent will linger. Your scent will mix with mine, and I'll have claimed you for my own." His lips brushed against her throat, and she shivered in response.

"Am I supposed to crave your bite," she asked breathlessly.

"Do you?" he asked softly.

"More than my next breath."

He chuckled. "As much as I want you to claim me it seems."

"And how does that work exactly?"

"Now that your wolf has been unleashed, your fangs will appear." He leaned in closer and kissed the bottom of her ear lobe. "While I'm inside you," he whispered the last part. "Toward the end they'll start throbbing, and you'll want to bite me…don't hesitate. Never deny your desire to touch me. I don't care if we're in the middle of the most prestigious ball in London, we *will* make our excuses and be off in an instant."

"The idea that I want you seems to drive you insane," she teased, as she ground against him.

"You have no damned idea," he hissed.

Amelia raised one eyebrow. "And then what happens?"

"You'll sink your fangs into my throat, and it'll be the most pleasurable experience you've ever had. The instant you break skin you'll complete your part of the bond. Your scent will mix with mine, and I'll belong to you."

"Only me," she growled possessively.

He chuckled. "I love when you do that."

"Do what?"

"Claim me. I have dreamt about this moment for years. I was sure it would never come, that you would be afraid of me and I would never again get to hold you like this after I told you the truth. It feels like a dream to be standing here with you, to hear you growl like that and know I'm not alone in this. The sounds you compose make my blood burn."

"I've never been jealous before, but since the beast made her appearance all I can think about is tying you to a bed somewhere and keeping you there forever."

"I can live that way." Laughter followed his words.

"Will it always be like this?"

"It'll calm a bit in a few years…but the inner desire for one another will always burn between us. It doesn't stop."

"Has it calmed for you?" she asked as she pulled his shirt up out of his breeches and slid her hand underneath the material and over his stomach.

He inhaled sharply. "Not even a little," he gasped as she ventured farther.

She scraped her nails across his chest gently and grinned at the soft moan that punctuated her ministrations.

"As many times as we have done this, I will never get used to your hands on me," he swore.

She slid her hand back down to graze the top of his breeches. She felt his muscles contract at her touch.

He fidgeted with the ties over her breasts and managed to open the bodice of her gown enough to sink his palm inside and cup her left breast. His thumb flicked over her nipple, and she gasped. "As much as I want to finish this…we're going to get caught," she purred.

"I'm almost willing to risk it." His words rasped against her ear, and Gideon dipped his head to kiss the top of her breasts. "Meet me tonight after the ball at our spot? I need to see you."

"You're seeing me now." She laughed at his words.

He feigned a pout. "Please, Amelia. I'm not ashamed to admit I'm desperate."

"How desperate?" she murmured, before slipping her fingers inside his waist band.

"I will do anything you want."

"Even that one with your tongue?"

His responding grin was confident. "*Especially* that one. You should have mentioned you liked it—it's my favorite too." He kissed her then, and retied the laces of her undergarments, effectively capturing her breasts in their casing once more. Amelia didn't remove her fingers from his breeches, but then he didn't seem to be in any hurry to get back to the ballroom either. She wanted more than anything for this moment to go on forever, but she knew it had to end soon. She pushed a little farther until she could touch the very top of him.

"You're killing me."

"Just giving you something to look forward to," she declared lightly, between kisses.

"Is that so?" He kissed her harder. His hand slid down her bodice to her hip, and lifted the skirt of her dress. The chemise hugging Amelia'a body didn't keep him from sliding his hand beneath. He traced her slit with his thumb, then dipped two fingers into her heat, teasing the sensitive nub as he stroked back and forth.

"That's…not….fair," she moaned breathlessly.

"All's fair in love, darling."

"I was teasing! You're…" She bit her lip on another faint mewl.

"Pleasuring you the way you deserve." He pressed faster, stroking her until her entire body shook with desire.

Amelia couldn't help herself—she yanked the back of his shirt from the waist band of his breeches and slipped her hands up the back of his shirt. She sank her nails into his skin, holding on for dear life, as he brought her closer and closer to the edge of reason.

Gideon nibbled her bottom lip, and the points of his fangs teased the sensitive flesh. He'd always hidden them before, she realized, but now with each tug of his teeth shocks of pleasure ricocheted through her body.

Her hips arched seemingly of their own accord, and she moved against his palm rhythmically. His free hand dropped to her hip, and then he pulled her as tightly as he could manage against his groin, and she rocked harder—unable to stop herself as his fingers moved faster. His breathing became labored, matching her breath for breath until she wasn't sure who was who. Finally, when she thought she could handle no more, she felt his fangs graze her throat, and she exploded.

Gideon's mouth covered hers, cutting off the rest of her cry of pleasure. Once her rocking slowed and then dwindled to a halt, he stepped back.

"You, my darling, would turn a saint into a sinner."

Amelia, still too dazed for proper words, mumbled incoherently.

"I didn't realize you would like my fangs so much."

She managed an amused huff. "This has possibilities."

His gaze leveled with hers suspiciously. "What sort of possibilities?"

"The kind in which I get to touch you without either of us getting caught with our pants down so to speak."

Her betrothed cursed. "Amelia, love, that was the sweetest, purest form of torture you could ever think to imagine. If you believe I'm going to let you repeatedly torment me that way without retaliating, you're insane."

"Maybe I look forward to your retaliation?" she teased.

"Sweet hell, your wolf is vicious." He grinned then. "She's going to get along perfectly with mine."

"It isn't just her, Gideon. If I thought I could get away with it, my skirts would be over my hips right now."

"The things I would do to you if I could. Just wait, love—a few more weeks, and you'll be mine," he vowed.

"You're already mine," she declared seductively.

He pulled her body roughly against his and kissed her hard. She kissed him back without hesitation, loving the feel of his mouth on hers entirely too much to care if they were caught in that moment. "And to think if I'd known how much you enjoyed me being possessive, we could have been doing this years ago."

"Apparently, we're not as good at communicating with each other as we thought," he conceded.

"Well." Amelia nodded in agreement. "We'll have to fix that, won't we?"

"In the meantime, one of us has to join the party before they notice we're missing.

"Oh." Amelia's one word showed her disappointment. "I would much rather continue what we were doing."

"Not if you don't want me to soil myself—which I haven't done since I was eighteen."

"What do you mean?"

"I need to compose myself, else every person in that ballroom will know what we've been doing out here."

"How do you have any self-control at all?" bemoaned Amelia softly.

"It's harder to control your natural urges when you're younger, and the wolf only makes things more difficult. We spent a lot of time together if you recall, so I had to learn to contain myself. The last time I lost control was the last year we were allowed in the swimming hole together."

She grinned nostalgically. "I'm not sure you're aware, but I did a bit of showing off to get your attention. It was at that time that I decided I no longer wanted to just be your friend. I was young, and foolish, and determined to get you to look at me differently. Clearly, I wasn't paying attention."

"Yes, well, it worked," he confessed. "Now, we need to get back to our guests. Are you going first or am I?"

Amelia suppressed a sigh, "I suppose we should, but won't they notice that…I—we?" She struggled to put her thoughts into words.

"No. They might assume I kissed you, but I will gladly take the responsibility." He grinned. "Always."

"Right. I will go first so you can regain your composure, but don't take too long. I'm sure both our parents are dying to announce our engagement. If you aren't there when the applause starts you needn't bother showing up at all." She smiled innocently. "Do we have an understanding?"

He laughed and pressed a kiss to her forehead. "I'll do my best, darling."

Amelia inhaled and held her breath in an attempt to gather her courage. She opened the door quietly and peeked in through the curtains. Satisfied no one loitered in the hall or was searching for her, she carefully slipped through the thick red curtains. The voices of the *guests* were inordinately loud, polluting the air with their meaningless chatter, and they seemed so much more vocal than she was used to, as if her hearing had suddenly become infinitely stronger than before. Perhaps it had. Then again, she'd never been able to hear a conversation from halfway across the room either. She was mere steps from the edge of the ballroom when she glanced self-consciously down at herself and managed to walk right into the back of one of the guests.

"I'm so sorry, forgive me," she gasped without bothering to see whom she'd bumped into.

"Please accept my apologies. I was looking for Lord Rochester. I'm Lord Cowen, Duke of Edington. You probably haven't heard of me, as I do not often appear at these types of events. May I ask who you are?"

"My father isn't here to introduce me...but I'm Lady Cavendash—a friend of the Rochester family. Soon to be the bride of the lord's son."

"Pity." He scowled at her, lifted his nose in disgust, and headed off in the opposite direction without so much as a farewell.

Amelia was momentarily shocked by his behavior, but then she shouldn't have been surprised. She'd always hated the *Ton*, and she couldn't think of a good reason to start admiring them now. Her thoughts on the unfortunate encounter were promptly set aside, however, as she heard Beatrix's voice. Amelia's focus shifted to find her friend chatting with Evangeline, a vicious curse they normally avoided at all costs— although chatting wasn't precisely the right word for what seemed to be happening.

Beatrix appeared to be ready to snap the other woman's head from her shoulders.

Evangeline, obviously unaware of the danger she was in, merely lifted her chin with a hoity sneer. "At her age I'm surprised he's interested in her at all. He must have grown tired of chasing the younger ladies and settled for someone more…*comfortable*."

"Lady Cavendash is a fine choice of a wife for any man, let alone the Duke of Rochester. They are a brilliant pair. You're just jealous that he didn't choose you. We're not blind, Lady Walch. We ladies have noticed your desperate attempts to get his and every other eligible bachelor's attention. Perhaps, it will be you who will be lucky enough to wrangle a husband. I do hope your invitation to their wedding is lost in the post, however."

Evangeline gasped. "And you, Lady Covington, you seem to be nearing the shelf as we speak. Do you have a conquest in mind? I can only imagine the desperation you should feel at *your* age."

Amelia's defenses rose, and she took a step forward away from the potted plant she'd been guarding yet again intending to intercede, only to have a soft female hand land on her shoulder.

"Leave it be, little one. Beatrix can handle the likes

of Lady Walch."

How did Gideon's mother always know when she needed her? Amelia's mother preferred to let her children make their own mistakes. She was a lovely caring mother, and they all adored her, but Lady Rochester always seemed to be near with sound advice whenever she was about to do something foolish—as if the woman understood her. Maybe she did, maybe because she'd been around so much for Amelia's childhood and because she was Gideon's mother, she knew more about Amelia than Amelia knew of herself. And for that, she was grateful.

"I see you found Gideon," she murmured when Amelia remained silent.

"Momentarily on the veranda." The heat rising in her cheeks stung her skin.

His mother smirked. "Yes, I'm sure. Gideon is my son, remember? I know him as well as I know you. I'd advise you two to make a stronger effort to keep your hands *and kisses* to yourself—lest your father changes his mind. I do want grandchildren someday. If it isn't too much to ask?"

Gideon was right. His mother assumed they had only been seeking stolen kisses. "I'm sorry."

"Don't be. You shouldn't be ashamed of your emotions, dear one. I'm quite pleased that you love my son so. It's any mother's dream for her children to feel the kind of love that only occurs once in a lifetime. I'm merely suggesting you don't get him killed. Your father is especially protective of his children. Much like we are of our own offspring. Have a care for my poor nerves?"

"Of course."

"Thank you." She smiled and nodded toward Beatrix, who had managed to free herself of Evangeline's clutches and was on her way to where they stood.

"*Pleaseeeee* do not invite that hateful hag to your wedding, Amelia. That woman is vile."

"I suspect my mother will be choosing the guest list, and she detests Lady Walch as much as most people. If Evangeline isn't careful, she's going to stop receiving calls at all. It would serve her right if the *Ton* gave her the cut direct," decided Amelia.

Beatrix smiled. "I knew there was a reason we're friends. Speaking of, Lady Rochester, I'm so glad Gideon has finally made Amelia an offer, and she's accepted at last." Beatrix beamed.

"Oh no. Surely, they would not have made the announcement without myself or Gideon being there?"

"No, dear heart, I spoke with your brother earlier," conceded Beatrix.

"Oh." Amelia sniffed delicately. The faintest hint of her brother's scent—a smell she'd only recently begun to recognize—perfumed the air between them. She glanced around curiously and found Parker on the other side of the room—too far for her to be able to smell him from the edge of the hallway. Her gaze darted back to Beatrix, who winked knowingly in response to Amelia's curious gaze.

"I assume you'll be announcing your own engagement soon, Beatrix," queried Gideon's mother, as if she could read Amelia's mind.

"One can only hope." Beatrix giggled out loud, before she flounced away as if everything she'd ever wanted had just been handed to her on a silver platter.

Amelia opened her mouth to respond, but no words came out.

"You can speak now," affirmed Lady Rochester. "She can't hear you from over there if you keep your voice down."

"She seems so proud of herself. Meanwhile I have had to hide my feelings. I don't understand."

"Beatrix is full-blooded, and she's been raised as a shifter. In our world, finding your mate is the epitome of success. Mates are rarer than you can imagine—most of our wolf kindred are not as fortunate. Your friend was raised to search for hers, which is why her parents aren't actively seeking her a husband. We may be members of the *Ton,* but we are shifters first. As I said before, most of us don't care whether or not you're half human. I'm sure her parents are as ecstatic that she's met your brother as we are about Gideon meeting you. However, you were raised as a human, and in such, you were brought up to keep your distance from men until you landed a husband."

"And yet my father and you still hold me to that standard despite my being *part*-human."

"You're absolutely correct. It's not an easy situation for any of us. We were expecting Gideon to marry you ages ago."

"It wasn't for lack of trying on his part, I assure you. I turned him down several times because he wasn't clear about his feelings. Feelings he couldn't freely express because of what he is and what he thought I was. I don't agree with the rule that half-blooded females should not know of their background unless they marry a shifter."

"Neither do I," agreed his mother. "And at any rate

it isn't a rule. It's a personal preference, which your parents made on your behalf. If you weren't aware of your inherited traits it was because your parents chose not to tell you, not because you weren't allowed to know."

"*If*? You knew I wasn't aware. You're friends with my parents, and you watched me grow up. I wouldn't have turned Gideon down so many times if I'd known!"

The duchess put her hand on Amelia's forearm gently. "A little louder, dear. I don't think everyone heard you."

Amelia purposely ignored her. She needed to speak to her parents. Alone. She could feel the wolf stirring as her temper rose and knew she needed to get away from the crowd before she really made a fool of herself, or worse, revealed her true nature. "Excuse me." She slid away from Lady Rochester and headed toward Gideon's study, making sure to keep to the edge of the ballroom and away from any prying busy bodies.

She walked down a secondary hall to outside the study door without any interruptions, thankfully. Amelia raised her hand to knock but stopped when she heard Gideon's father speaking to her parents.

"I'm sorry, but did you honestly think this wouldn't happen eventually? You've known for fourteen years they were mates. How long did you expect him to stay away from her?"

Amelia was afraid to get any closer, afraid they would pick up on her scent, but more than anything she needed to hear their conversation.

"Of course, I knew! I'm not blind. You told me yourself," growled her father. "Society nonsense aside, she is my daughter, and we're not of the same pack, so therefore he should have made a formal request to court her."

"*That* is society nonsense! It is not our way. Gideon followed every shifter law. He hasn't marked her, and he hasn't kidnapped her. He did what is natural to us. You can't fault him for doing what a mate would."

"She is still my daughter, Roderick!"

"I'm aware, and again, I'm sorry, but he didn't do anything wrong!"

Amelia heard her father sigh. "You're right."

"You wear hunter's musk—that mixture your brother concocted to hide your scent, and you asked us not to tell our children that you're one of us. We yielded to your request, so Gideon wouldn't have known she was a half-blood. If he had known you were one of us from the start this would have been settled years ago. If you had told your daughters, this would not have happened at all."

"If their mates aren't shifters, they won't be able to unlock their wolf. There is no need to involve them in our world if they're to remain unchanged."

"I respect your right to raise your family as you deem fit, but I don't agree. Amelia isn't just your family anymore. She has been ours too. You know this is true, just as you also knew she would unlock her wolf. Keeping secrets from us is one thing, but you should have told *her* at the very least. Now he has to, and it could affect their bonds if she doesn't accept her true nature. She might be afraid of him—she might reject him. Or worse, she could tell someone the truth about us, and they would have her committed. Then what do you suspect might happen? If the others don't have her killed to keep her quiet, my son would have to abandon his own pack, and take her away from here. You put both of their lives at risk!"

"She didn't show any interest in him until recently," balked Amelia's father.

"Are you blind? They have been inseparable! Even as children they were always together!"

"But she didn't see him as anything more than a friend."

Amelia couldn't take any more. She pushed the door open, walked inside, and then silently closed it behind her. She didn't want anyone else wandering by and hearing the conversation. Well, at least a human wouldn't be able to hear through the thick, heavy wood.

Her parents faced her in surprise as she steadily made her way across the room toward them, and she lifted her chin proudly—painfully aware that what she was about to say might hurt them.

"You are wrong." She struggled deeply to gather what remained of her courage. "What you're doing is *wrong*. Mother might be human, but you are not." She sent her father a sidelong glimpse of frustration.

He opened his mouth, but she held up her hand.

"I mean absolutely no disrespect. You are my parents, and I love you, but this is *wrong*. I'm not normal, and I never will be. Even without Gideon, I don't want a human's life! I don't want to marry some boring duke and follow the *Ton*'s dreadful rules. I don't want to attend humdrum functions and listen to horrid musicals. I don't want to bear children and hand them off to nannies to be raised *properly*. I am unwed, not because I haven't had offers…Gideon himself has proposed to me at least twenty times!"

She raised her hand toward the door in emphasis. "I know you haven't been able to speak to Parker yet, but I am not even like you. I'm an Omega. Gideon didn't need to mark me to unleash my wolf—she's already there. And likely my sisters are too! You shouldn't have kept us from knowing who we are. Gideon could never tell me the truth unless we were married, so I didn't know how he really felt. But if you had told me the truth, I could have married him eight years ago when I lost my virginity to him!"

She crossed her arms. "And it wasn't his fault—I wasn't innocent either. I've had feelings for him since I was fifteen. The *Ton* says I should be pristine and pure for my husband, but as a female wolf there would have been nothing wrong with me pursuing him. Parker's mate is a full-blood, and no one has tried to shame her for being too near him. I'm no different than she is. I shouldn't have to hide how I feel from my family." She swiped at a stray tear that had found its way down her cheek and did her best to ignore her father's heart-broken expression.

"I love him, and I have for so long. He's my best friend, and the only person who's ever been completely honest with me. If you need to blame someone for the loss of my innocence, blame yourself for not telling me the truth. Blame me for not caring about society's ludicrous restrictions. But don't blame him for following his instincts, and don't blame Gideon for not denying his true nature."

"Amelia—"

"Honestly, Father, if it wasn't for Gideon I would probably be dead by now. You tried to tell me beasts didn't exist. You made me feel like a lunatic for believing in them, and I sought them out to prove to myself that I wasn't insane. Gideon found me out there alone, hunting them. If not for him there's a real chance I would have found one, and I could have been another missing girl. We're in here arguing over something so trivial as my virtue when there are women being kidnapped by rogue wolves. This is ridiculous! I gave my innocence to Gideon, and I don't regret doing so one bit. I would do it again without hesitation. Your strength and time would be better spent on something more important like finding those girls. *Now*, I love you, and I'm sorry for the way I've spoken to you. I know it was rude. But I'm going to marry Gideon before the season is over. And despite how our betrothal came about, I hope you'll come to the wedding."

She dried her eyes once more, and confident that she was presentable, she hugged her mother and kissed her cheek. "I apologize for my tone. I know you don't believe a lady should raise her voice," she whispered, though she knew everyone else heard as well.

Amelia offered her father an apologetic smile. "I know you mean well." Then she turned to the current duke of Rochester, Gideon's father, and clasped her hands before her shamefully. "I hope you know I would never intentionally hurt your son." She didn't wait for a response before offering a timid smile and without another word left—making certain to close the door behind her on her way out. Once in the hallway, she froze in mortification when she realized her tantrum had drawn an audience.

Standing around looking guilty were her brother, Parker, Gideon's mother, Beatrix, Beatrix's father, and even Gideon.

"I don't suppose you've only just arrived and missed that spectacle?" Amelia asked softly, her voice cracking in humiliation.

Gideon stood near the back of the group, his arms crossed while he leaned against the wall, looking as handsome as ever. Her mate looked as if he might be beaming.

Parker cleared his throat. "I told Hannah and Poppy. I don't know if Father would agree, but he's already announced he's stepping down as our alpha in a few weeks, and since I'll be taking his seat, I thought it only fair. You were right. They should know—you deserved to know. I'm sorry I never told you."

She sent her brother a weak smile. "Thank you."

He nodded.

"I know I have told you this before since we're friends, but I absolutely adore you," gasped Beatrix with a broad grin. "You are an inspiration! I hope to be an alpha as strong as you someday!" She flung her arms around Amelia and squeezed hard enough to crack ribs.

Beatrix finally released her, and without waiting for an invitation, Amelia threw her arms around Gideon's mother.

"Thank you for everything you've done for me," she whispered.

Lady Rochester hugged her back. "I did nothing, dear one. I told you, you are never less than you are."

Amelia shook her head, letting the tears stinging her eyes fall as she held onto the older woman. "You did much more. You taught Gideon I was enough the way I am."

"My son may be stubborn, but he is not stupid."

Lady Rochester tittered. "I didn't need to tell him." She released Amelia. "Now, excuse me. Your father might not be happy with all this, but he knows you're right about those missing girls, and I thought Lord Covington would benefit from a meeting with your parents and my husband." She smiled kindly and led Beatrix's father into the study.

Beatrix clapped her hands. "This is going to be so fantastic." She kissed Parker quickly on the cheek, then skipped back down the hall toward the ballroom.

Parker sighed. "Thankfully she doesn't have a brother to land me a facer," he admitted remorsefully. He glanced at Gideon. "Sorry about that."

Gideon shrugged. "No harm done."

Her brother took his leave, abandoning her into Gideon's sole care.

Amelia knew Gideon was dying to respond, but she didn't want to hear anything he had to say when her parents might hear it also. It was most likely going to be something incredibly private, and she wanted to keep what little remained of her pride.

"I need a moment before I'm forced back into the ballroom. Perhaps you could give me a brief tour of your home," she asked hopefully.

"That can be arranged, but I want you to know how much I appreciate your words." Gideon grinned empathetically. "Right this way, milady." He held out his arm, and she took it gratefully. "Just to be clear, however, this is *our* home, or it will be soon. I hope you will like it here."

****

Gideon led his betrothed down the halls of his home, and he couldn't help but look at her with each corner they turned. More than anything he wanted her to love her new home as much as he loved her. He wanted—no *needed* Amelia to be happy with him.

After everything he'd just heard her admit, he was confident that he had the situation well in hand. She was beautiful and so brave! As an alpha, he'd considered himself strong, but his strength was nothing in comparison to his mate's. She had defended him against her parents, when she didn't have to. It warmed his heart to hear her speak so highly of him, and even more to see her forge a deeper bond with his parents. It was a good sign that she truly was content with him.

He watched her face light up as she noticed odd bobbles around the house, items he no longer paid attention to. Like the tiny stone wolf his mother had purchased in a shop guarding the doorway of some random room he hardly used. Amelia noticed everything, and he couldn't stop staring as she seemed to transform in front of him. She was a rare bloom finally opening after years of patient tending, and he couldn't believe he would finally see her blossom after over a decade of biding his time.

Her eyes glittered with interest, and his heart beat rapidly in response. His amazing, courageous, passionate bride-to-be with her quick wit and fiery temper. Admittedly enamored, he couldn't wait to wake up next to her each morning. Yet, Gideon knew he had more pressing matters just then. He should have been in the study with his father, debating their next steps to find the missing girls. He should have been planning an attack on the rogues threatening his city. He certainly shouldn't have been escorting Amelia farther and farther away from the ball unchaperoned—not when both sets of parents were preparing to announce their engagement. But he couldn't help himself. He was doing everything he could for the missing girls, and he trusted his father to handle the meeting with Beatrix's father.

Tonight, he wanted to put aside his duties and for one instance just be in love and not have to worry about the pack. This evening, he wanted to dedicate his time to his mate and experience what it was like to spend a leisurely evening with her. There were so many things he still didn't know about her, even after all these years, and he wanted to know everything. This evening was about her, because tomorrow his attention would be on the missing females and the rogues who thought to invade neutral territory.

Tomorrow he had to be an alpha. Tonight, he would be simply a mate.

Chapter Seven

"What was it like as a child, knowing I was your mate?"

Amelia sat comfortably on the edge of a plump settee staring into the soft crackling flames of a fireplace. They were in a second smaller study on the other side of the house. This one was more impersonal with an empty desk and a few bookshelves but little else. Behind her, Gideon stood on the other side of the divan. His hands kneaded her shoulders rhythmically in a relaxing motion that would have her asleep within the hour if she didn't stop him.

"It's not exactly the same as what we have now," he explained softly.

"It must have been strange."

He chuckled. "Not at all. I have been a shifter my entire life. I had been taught what to expect. Granted, I thought I would be an adult when it happened. It was frustrating, but not in the way you imagine. At fourteen I was still a child in some ways, and you were younger than I was. You were nice, and you played children's games with me."

"Except for the time you shoved me in the mud after I broke your doll. That was unexpected, but it only made me like you more. You weren't afraid of me, and I had been taught that humans would despise us if they knew what we really were. I only wanted to talk to you and tell you all my secrets. I felt like I could trust you. Then as we got older, and our games matured, you didn't talk about marrying a man with a title like the other girls your age did.

"You didn't imagine grand weddings or flirt with stable hands as some ladies do. I was relieved. When you were sixteen and made your debut, I debated telling you how I felt, but it seemed too soon. I was afraid you'd hate me if you knew the truth. So, I started bribing your would-be suitors and paying off fortune hunters. It was a bit difficult then because our peers had become active in society, and I wanted so badly to court you. I wasn't allowed to be alone with you anymore because we were of age, and I had to invent ways to see you."

Amelia smiled. "I remember when I met you. My parents were having a soiree for my twelfth birthday and had invited all our neighbors. I had never met your family before that day, but when you first approached me you asked how old I was, and when I told you, you said, *that's only two years, I can marry you after you turn seventeen. You'll be my wife someday.* It was the oddest thing I'd ever heard. I thought you were so funny, and suddenly I needed you to be my friend. No one had ever talked to me like that—so honestly. My father spent a lot of time with my brothers, and they always seemed to know things I didn't and would never answer my questions. But you always did. Even a week ago, in the graveyard, I told you I was hunting beasts, and you blurted out the truth just like you did when we were children." She sighed. "I love that about you."

"I remember a few days after my eighteenth birthday when we were in the garden. I told you I had found a book under my brother's bed—the one depicting naked Greek statues, and I wanted to know if a man sincerely appeared the same underneath his clothes as they did in the images. You didn't want to answer, but you did anyway, and when I didn't believe you, I called you a liar, and you asked if I wanted to see the truth for myself…who knew that innocent comment would lead to so much more?"

"It would have been fine if you hadn't asked to touch me.*"*

Amelia giggled faintly, and her entire body seemed to melt into the divan as she faded more and more into blissful content. She stifled a yawn and tried to keep her eyes from closing. It had been a long day. "I was never terribly brave except with you. You've always helped me feel so sure of myself."

"Why me? The mating bond is a lot of things, but it doesn't control how we feel about each other."

She shifted into a more comfortable position across the back of the settee and snuggled into the cushion, forcing Gideon to lose his grip on her shoulders. She yawned yet again, and her eyelashes fluttered.

"When I was thirteen, you told me that as long as I was with you, I could do whatever I wanted. That you would protect me. Since then I have always felt confident when you were close by. Even when I was older and understood the world better, I felt the same way. I trusted you."

"I hope you always feel that way," he whispered. Gideon's lips gently caressed her cheek. She hadn't been sleeping well, and the events of the night had stolen what little energy remained. Despite her desire to stay awake and talk to her beloved, she couldn't conquer the lure of slumber.

****

Gideon grinned when he heard his mate's delicate snoring. She was beautiful under the glow of the flames dancing in the fireplace, her flesh like porcelain, and he wanted to trace every curve, but for once, he forced himself to keep his hands away from her. He continued to watch her sleep, until he felt his own eyelids droop. He should have taken her back to the ballroom. He certainly shouldn't have kept her away for so long—no doubt her parents were looking for her.

The duke would hunt him down and execute him if he knew Gideon was hoarding her like a precious gem—unchaperoned. And he would take the punishment. It would be worth it to know she rested peacefully because of him. She didn't understand the effect she had on him, and somehow that made it all the more magical. He wanted nothing more than to lie with Amelia, holding her in his arms and in his bed for the rest of the night. But he couldn't dishonor her pack that way. He'd been careful to keep with traditions, albeit not the human ones, but the ones shape-shifters held to, and he wasn't going to let all his carefully laid plans go to waste now. She deserved a proper mating, and he would make sure she had one.

Neither did Gideon have the heart to wake her, but he also couldn't bring himself to send for her brothers. Instead, he lifted her into his arms and held her tightly against his chest. Her soft body lay flushed against his, and for once, he wasn't burning with desire. For once it was only his heart that flamed with a feverish need.

Asleep, she looked pure and angelic, like a goddess from one of the books Parker collected. Her eyelashes fluttered as he carried her from the room, and he prayed he wouldn't meet anyone in the hall. Once in his bedroom, he closed the door carefully behind them with his foot and laid her gently on the bed, and then pulled the blankets up over her shoulders.

It took every bit of willpower he had not to slide into the bed next to her, but he forced himself to walk away. He swore to himself for being honorable. The pianofortes were no longer playing as he headed back toward the ballroom, and Gideon was much relieved to find most of the guests had gone. His sisters still entertained a few stragglers. One in particular he recognized as Lord Cowen, who seemed particularly reluctant to leave. Parker and the rest of the Cavendash brood had disappeared—all but Amelia's father,who sat next to Gideon's own—nursing a glass of brandy as if they had nothing better to do.

Lord Cavendash's gaze swung to meet Gideon's the instant he was within sight, and Gideon immediately threw up his hands in defense as he approached the older wolf. "I swear I did not touch her," he vowed.

"Even by our standards, you can't just sneak off with a man's daughter and not expect him to meet you at forty paces," growled Lord Cavendash.

Gideon nodded. "Please accept my humblest apologies. I meant no harm. She was tired, and I didn't have the heart to make her go back into the ballroom."

"Have a heart. You and I were no better at his age. Your mate's father nearly shot you dead in a field when he caught you sneaking around with his daughter," divulged Gideon's father.

Lord Cavendash snorted. "That was before I had a

daughter of my own."

Gideon's father nodded in agreement. "Daughters." He sighed. "Have no fear, Gideon will respect your wishes. He'll stay in a guest room, and you can sleep in the one next to Amelia."

"Like bloody hell. I'm sleeping outside her door. I remember what you were like, Roderick, and I'm not going to trust your spawn to avoid temptation. Don't forget—I was barely an adult when I arrived in London all those years ago, and you were my first friend. You helped me counterfeit my brother's position as the Duke of Cavendash, and in return I swore to be your ally always. We have been through it all together— vampires, witches, but none of it compared to meeting our mates. There's something about those bonds that will make a man do the most foolish things. When you left to search for your mate, I stayed behind to guard your territory just as I promised. I was still here all those years later when you finally decided to return with your own family in tow. So if you think there's a prayer of me letting my guard down any time before the wedding, you've lost your mind. Maybe I can't control Amelia, but I can make damn sure your son doesn't have an easy time of getting close to her. After all, don't I recall you mentioning he was nearly born out of wedlock?"

"You have my word," vowed Gideon.

"Your word is about as good as your father's was when he promised your grandfather your mother would be a virgin on their wedding day. We might be loyal, but when it comes to our mates, all bets are off. You won't be joining her again tonight, boy." Lord Cavendash rose with a sigh. "We'll discuss the matter of the missing females in more depth tomorrow. I still think we need to increase our search outside the territory. It's likely the rogues are holding them just out of your boundaries, where we can't sense them."

Gideon nodded. "I agree." He watched his mate's father shuffle down through the hall in exhaustion and turned to face his own father. "I swear I didn't touch her."

"Soon enough, son. You'll be mated in less than a month, and this will all be behind us."

"I'll be mated, but those women will still be missing." Gideon joined his father near the liquor cart and lowered his voice, "The sooner I'm mated, the sooner my beast will let me focus on finding them. As long as I can't touch her, it's hard as hell to focus on anything else."

His father nodded knowingly. "You're no different than any other male who's found his mate, and we have all been there. You've had to wait a bit longer than usual, but no one blames you, even her father. He's just being protective. You'll see when you have daughters of your own."

Gideon watched his father amble across the ballroom to dismiss the remainder of the guests. It had been a long night, and they had not been able to announce the engagement.

Lord Cowen—a fellow wolf, seemed to protest the loudest as Lord Rochester led him to the door.

Gideon shook his head. Some men would do anything for a free drink.

****

How dare that insolent toddler dismiss him! Edgar paced the length of his study. His hands rested behind his back—holding himself in check as he thought through his next move. All he could see was red—his mind clouded with blood lust, but he wasn't yet so far gone that he couldn't plot his next attack. Already he had a couple of females, but he needed more. He needed her.

Edgar considered going after the wench himself, and he'd planned the perfect abduction!

He would snatch her right out from under her family's nose and lead them back to the rogues, throwing them off his scent and giving him time to get away with his new mate in tow. It was a perfect plan, except that there were too many variables. He couldn't have the wolves chasing his scent, so it couldn't be him who snatched her like a thief in the night. He needed a scapegoat—someone smart enough to get away, but too stupid to realize Edgar's true motives. He had the rogues at his disposal, but only one of them could pull it off. The others were about as mindless as the animals they turned into. He'd order the bloodthirsty mongrel to bring the female to him, and then he'd sacrifice his budding pack to the London wolves who'd no doubt trail the rogue back to the den.

Edgar didn't mind sacrificing the other women if it meant he'd have his chosen mate, but he was loath to give up on them just yet. There was still time for him to have it all, but more importantly, he had to get *her* away from her family before it was too late. He could sense time was running out, and the beast in him raged at the thought of losing his female.

Sharp canines exploded from his gums as his body threatened to shift into his wolf without Edgar's consent. He could feel his own darkness creeping into his mind, reminding him of the taste of blood—a sustenance he craved and one which drove him to hunt yet another unsuspecting human. He wanted so badly to give in to the lust, and he would once he had the female, but until then, he clenched his fists, drawing blood and pain from his palms where his nails pierced the skin, distracting him from the addiction he'd fought off for so long. While in London he must maintain his Lordly persona.

Just a little longer, he consoled himself. He envisioned her locked within his grasp and the beast in him momentarily subdued. He was so close he could almost taste her, but she remained just out of his reach, taunting his wolf, and forcing Edgar to move forward with his plan before he was ready. Tonight, he would send one of the imbecile rogues after her, and with any luck he'd be well on his way to Glasgow with his future wife by morning.

Chapter Eight

Amelia woke the next morning with a keen realization that she was *not* in her own bed. She glanced around, trying her best to recognize anything. She vaguely remembered falling asleep on the chaise in Gideon's second study, but after that, nothing. Now she reclined in a large four-poster bed with sheets that were vastly different than the rose-colored ones that covered her own smaller bed. The windows were large, covered by thick, dark-green curtains, almost the same shade as the sheets, and the room was clean and bare of any personal effects. For a moment she panicked, and then she took a deep breath, pulling the room's scents into her nostrils. This was Gideon's room.

She sniffed the pillows experimentally, grinning as his masculine scent continued to invade her senses. All at once she felt safe.

Amelia rose from the bed with a smile, despite the fact that she was still dressed in her ball gown—not the most comfortable thing to sleep in, even though her stays had clearly come undone. Birds chirped outside the window, and the faintest beams of sunlight streamed in between the curtains where they didn't quite meet in the middle. She couldn't help but wonder why her parents had left her here to begin with. Surely, after all the fuss her father had made, he would not condone her spending the night in Gideon's home, let alone his bed, without a chaperone. She retied her stays, straightened her gown, and went to the door—curious to see what had transpired. She cautiously pulled the heavy door open, and then howled with laughter.

Lying on the floor with nothing but a pillow and blanket for comfort, her father was sound asleep in the doorway—still dressed in his evening clothes. As she continued to be consumed by amusement, he stirred and grunted, his eyes opened, and he saw her standing over him. "I am not as young as I used to be," he groused in response to her merriment.

"What on earth is going on?"

"Roderick's boy moved you into his chamber last night. After the way the day had gone, and Parker's explanation of what happened earlier, we thought it was better to let you rest. But I wasn't about to let that boy sneak in here, so Parker took your mother and the girls home."

"And you guarded the door." Amelia swallowed anxiously. "What about the announcement, since we weren't there will you and Mother…"

"Yes, well, your mother has decided to host a ball this weekend, and we'll announce it then. Now…my back hurts, and I'm hungry. If you're presentable, I'm ready to get on with the day."

Amelia nodded tearfully. Even after everything, her father still only wanted the best for her. He got to his feet, and she threw her arms around him.

"I'm sorry for the way I acted last night."

"You have every right to be angry. Your mother and I were just trying to protect you, and we made a mess of things. Or rather, I did. Your mother thought we should tell you girls the truth. I'm sorry I made things harder for you and…"

"His name is Gideon."

Her father cleared his throat. "*That boy*. Anyway, I just thought you should know."

"Thank you, Father. I know you meant well." She released her grip and smiled warmly up at him.

He linked his arm in hers. "I want my breakfast," he huffed, ignoring her praise. "Shall we?"

****

Gideon cursed as he studied the riverbank. He couldn't *see* them, but he could smell the decaying bodies. The scent of dead fish and molded wood made excellent camouflage, he had to admit, and if he was a rogue dining on innocent people, this would've been a perfect spot unless another wolf happened by. But the rogues terrorizing both humans and wolves were not nearly as far gone mentally as he'd imagined. Not with finding such a perfect location for those they had slain. Of course, it didn't matter—despite what degree their minds had or had not deteriorated to, a rogue was still a rogue in every aspect of the word—smart or not, dark or not. The rules for their kind insisted and rightly so that anyone who feasted on human-flesh had to be captured and put down.

Understanding of a rogue's state of mind only made Gideon realize how severe the infestation had grown. It wouldn't be as simple as hunting down a snarling blood crazed wolf as he had the last rogue. The ones he and the London wolves hunted would be harder to catch, which meant he would lose more female wolves and certainly more humans to the rogues' insatiable appetite before it was over.

His heart ached to imagine the people who'd died,

123

and the horrors they had certainly endured. The missing female wolves were still unaccounted for, but in his gut he knew they were getting closer. Unfortunately, he *had* found some of the missing humans, and thankfully there would be no bodies to dispose of this time. While the Thames River claimed their corpses, their deaths couldn't be linked back to his packmates—a bittersweet mercy that allowed him to continue focusing on the missing girls.

The rogues were getting bolder. It was only a matter of time before they exposed his kind's existence to the human population. There'd be another witch hunt, but it wouldn't be the magically inclined that suffered—it would be Gideon's friends and family. They would be hunted like dogs and tortured relentlessly—all because he couldn't locate the damned rogues. His inner beast demanded to be released, but Gideon kept a careful leash on the wolf. They couldn't hunt in the city, and especially not during broad daylight. It was too dangerous. He'd left his mate alone with his family, but already the need to get back to her and make sure she was safe was paramount. He stared out over the river for a little longer, letting his gaze patrol the bank suspiciously, as if one of the rogues might simply happen by on a morning stroll. He knew he couldn't get that lucky, but his need to protect Amelia from the threat of rogue wolves took precedence over surveying the river, and soon he was on his way home once more. Where hopefully the dread he felt was merely in response to the missing girls and not a premonition of things to come.

****

Gideon was out. Searching for the missing girls

according to his mother when Amelia and her father made their goodbyes. Amelia wasn't disappointed. She was glad he cared enough to try and find them. It didn't matter that she didn't know the women—they were innocent and in danger, and they needed help.

She wished she could join the hunt. But never would Gideon, her father, or her brothers allow her to do so. The rogues were much too dangerous, especially since she had never shifted completely.

They arrived home in short order, and she had just enough time to change into a more comfortable dress before all hell broke loose.

"What do you mean, she's gone?"

Amelia rushed down the stairs at the sound of her father's furious tone. "Who's gone?" she demanded breathlessly.

"Lizbeth," admitted her mother, her voice and expression filled with concern.

"You don't think she ran off with Lunsford's son do you?" queried Hadley.

"I'll kill him," swore her father.

"He just turned eighteen, and she won't be sixteen until next week. They are barely old enough to get married in Gretna Green," argued Parker. "I don't understand. She was in Amelia's bed asleep last night. I checked before I went to bed."

"Well she isn't here now," snapped their father. "You were supposed to look after them and so far, you've failed! You let that one run wild with Rochester's boy—" He threw his hand up in Amelia's direction. "—and now you've lost another! I shouldn't even leave Hannah and Poppy in your care."

"Henry," chastised their mother. "Amelia isn't a

child any longer. You knew Gideon had been following her, and you're the one who didn't tell them. What's worst is that you knew about the rogues and missing girls, and yet you still brought Lizbeth to town!"

"I didn't have a choice! Lunsford refused to stay in the country!"

"You brought Lizbeth to London because of Lunsford's son, but you wouldn't tell Amelia about Gideon," accused Parker, agreeing with his mother.

"I didn't tell Lizbeth why we came to London either, *you* did!"

Amelia swallowed anxiously. "Stop arguing! It doesn't matter. Lizbeth is gone, and we should be looking for her, not standing here bickering over whose fault it is."

"She's right, Henry. We need to call on Lunsford. Maybe he knows where she's gone," agreed Amelia's mother frantically.

"That boy is dead," vowed her father.

Amelia watched as her mother and father hurriedly left the house. She prayed they found Lizbeth with Lunsford's son, but she suspected something far more sinister.

"What if she isn't with Lunsford?" hissed Hadley after they'd gone.

"Don't say it," snapped Parker. "Don't you dare say it. She *has* to be with Lunsford—if the rogues got to her…" He shuddered. "We need to take the girls to Gideon's for now, so we can help look for Lizbeth. It isn't safe here until we know what happened."

"Gideon isn't home," admitted Amelia.

"It doesn't matter. He has too many cousins to count. It's far safer for you and our sisters to be with his family where there are plenty of eyes to watch over you. Pack an overnight bag. I don't know how long this will take."

Within the hour Amelia found herself once more on Gideon's doorstep.

Parker's fist pounded heavily on the townhouse door, and Gideon's manservant let them in immediately.

"What's wrong, what has happened?" demanded Lord Rochester the instant he saw them in his entryway.

"My sister Lizbeth has gone missing. I was hoping I could leave the girls here. My home isn't safe right now," explained Parker briefly.

"Of course." Rochester nodded. "I'll call the rest of the boys in. Let me get my jacket, and I'll help you look. Where do you think she's gone?"

Parker followed Rochester out of the room, and Amelia ushered her sisters into the drawing room, followed by Lady Rochester.

"Gideon should be home any minute. Make yourself comfortable. I'll ring for tea."

Amelia nodded. She watched her sisters take a seat near the fireplace—their expressions, nearly identical, were composed of shock and dismay. They hadn't said anything yet, but she knew there was more worrying them than Lizbeth's absence. Parker had told them the truth last night, and she wondered if that had something to do with it as well. Now was not the time to approach the topic, but she promised herself she'd have a talk with them later. She was the oldest sister and owed them that much.

"Your mother mentioned Lunsford's son had imprinted on her…do you think she's there? Sixteen is a terrible age to discover your wolf. You're already emotional and headstrong, and everything is intensified," said Gideon's mother a moment later after her return.

"We hope that's where she is…" Amelia allowed her words to fade away. She didn't want to think of the possible alternative.

"But you don't think so." Lady Rochester lifted her chin and inhaled sharply. "The rogues?"

"If it was, they are terribly bold. Whomever took Lisbeth came to our house and snatched her from my bed. Why wouldn't they take Hannah or Poppy too?"

"There are only a few rogues from what I've gathered. They wouldn't be able to take that many at once. Lizbeth is the youngest and the weakest, and she's also the same age as the other girls who were taken," explained Lady Rochester.

"But why?"

"Rogues are immoral creatures, Amelia. They don't need a reason to do what they do. They lose all of their ability to account for their actions once the blood rage sets in."

"What's blood rage?"

"It's what happens to a shifter without a mate. Maybe their mate died—it's hard to say," sighed Lady Rochester.

"Could that have happened to Gideon? If I had truly rejected him?"

The duchess nodded. "It could happen to any of us. With mates, however, once you're bonded, you can't be separated. If one dies, so does the other. In order to become a rogue, you would have never had the bonds. So it could be, they went too long without finding their mate, or they lost them before they could mark them as their own."

"What about Hannah and Poppy? Our father wasn't going to tell any of us…could we have gone rogue as well?"

"Theoretically yes, but you're an Omega, and Omegas don't go rogue. They aren't susceptible to the blood rage like the rest of us."

"But he didn't know that."

Gideon's mother shrugged. "It usually takes a long while, sometimes hundreds of years. Without their mate, a half-blood typically dies a human death."

"So, he thought we would just marry human men and die?"

"That is what happens, Amelia. It's harder for half-bloods, and that's why there used to be laws against shifters mating humans. But we were losing too many to the blood rage, and they lifted the law. That's what started the snubbing of half-bloods to begin with."

"But if I hadn't been an Omega, and I had rejected Gideon and died a normal death, he could have become a rogue?"

Lady Rochester nodded. "Yes."

"And my parents knew this."

Gideon's mother bit her lip as if she didn't want to answer the question. "It's different for everyone, Amelia. You have to understand they were just protecting you."

"But they were risking Gideon."

"He's our son, not theirs. He's in our pack. They don't have to be concerned about his welfare."

"But they love him."

"Yes, but they didn't know you would accept him.

They hold your welfare above his. You're their daughter, and that's normal. They never decreed that Gideon couldn't court you, only that he couldn't tell you the truth until he married you."

"How did they know that he was a wolf? Gideon didn't know we were half-bloods."

"Your father wears hunter's musk. It camouflages his scent. He preferred we didn't tell our children the truth, and we respected his wishes. But he could still scent Gideon, and your father knew what *we* were. We told Gideon that we had revealed our nature to your father years earlier.

"Gideon's father and yours were young boys together during school, and friends for many years before you were born. It wasn't a lie. Usually, when shape-shifters meet, they're able to detect each other's nature due to their scent, and Gideon would've easily discovered the truth if your father hadn't been actively trying to hide his true nature from the rest of London.

"He explained that he thought it would be safer for your family that way, and as half-blooded shifters don't carry the same distinctive scent—Gideon wouldn't have realized. We had to respect his decision, but it wasn't easy for us to hide the truth from our children, especially after Gideon recognized his connection to you. After Gideon's father and I married, we lived near my parents for a time, before we decided to strike out and build our own pack.

"After a while we made our way back here so our children would have an easier time finding their mates, as London is most commonly referred to as the marriage mart of England. We reunited with your family—I believe that was the year you turned twelve, and we realized you were Gideon's destined mate. We told our son as much of the truth as we could, but we obviously left out a few key details."

"But Gideon could have become a rogue," insisted Amelia.

"I understand your frustration, Amelia."

"Do you?" Amelia shook her head, dismissing the horrifying thought of Gideon becoming a rogue. "We need to focus on finding my sister and the other girls. We'll worry about everything else later. Hannah and Poppy now know what they are. Lizbeth knows also, at least there's that."

Amelia heard the front door open and close.

"Mother?" Gideon entered the room and paused upon seeing them. "Amelia?" His eyes lit up with the glow she loved when he saw her. "I thought your father would have you home by now." He started toward Amelia, but spotted Hannah and Poppy near the fireplace and hesitated. "Is anything wrong?"

His mother dismissed herself quietly, and Amelia sighed.

"We can't be certain, but we think rogues took Lizbeth. She's missing."

He swallowed. "They took her from where, Amelia?"

"Our home."

"Is it possible she snuck out to see Lunsford's son?"

Amelia shrugged. "My parents, brothers, and your father went to find out. And before that he called your cousins to come here. Parker didn't want to leave us home alone."

"Good, that's perfect. You'll be safe." He lifted his

palm to her cheek. "I need to talk to you alone."

Amelia glanced at her sisters, who still hadn't acknowledged the situation. Gideon's mother stood nearby, and the woman inclined her head, acknowledging Amelia's silent request and went back into the drawing room to sit with them.

"What is it?" she asked after Gideon led her into his study.

"We found one of the girls."

She waited for him to say something else, and when he didn't she realized why. Her breath sawed in and then out, her mind racing a mile a minute. "How long was she missing?"

"A couple of weeks."

She nodded. "Then there's a chance Lizbeth is all right," she whispered more to herself.

"There's always a chance, Amelia. We won't stop looking until we find her. I swear."

"Gideon, there's something else."

"What?"

"Lizbeth was in my bed last night when they took her. What if they weren't looking for Lizbeth? What if they wanted me?"

"It has to be a coincidence." He grabbed her and pulled her into his arms.

"What if it's because I was in the graveyard that night? Maybe they followed me home. What if I led them to her?"

"Stop. You can't think like that. Rogues don't have the ability to reason. If they followed you, they would have taken you the instant I was gone. I didn't sense anyone else in the graveyard that night. I would have known."

"Maybe she did just sneak out. Maybe she is with Lunsford's son. She wouldn't be the first Cavendash woman to sneak out to meet a boy," she mumbled darkly.

Gideon chuckled and hugged her tighter.

"You're all right though, aren't you, Gideon? My rejections didn't affect you. You're not going to turn into a rogue, are you?"

He kissed the top of her head. "No, my love. I'm fine. I was disappointed, but not defeated. I still had faith you'd come around. A rogue is what happens to a shifter who's lost all hope of finding their mate. I found you, that was the hard part." He kissed her head once more. "I think I hear my cousins. Come, I want them to meet my mate."

Suddenly anxious all over again, she let Gideon pull her from the room and into the entry where a handful of males were filing in with several more behind them. They all looked up upon Gideon's arrival, and multiple pairs of eyes dropped to her hand clasped in his.

"So, this is the mystery woman," chirped one of his cousins.

Amelia recognized him from the ball where she'd first tried to end her relationship with Gideon.

"Tristan, this is Amelia, Lady Cavendash—my mate."

Gideon's cousin whistled. "No wonder you weren't interested in Lady Walch."

Amelia couldn't help it—she scowled.

Tristan laughed. "Excuse my manners. It's been a long night. I was on patrol looking for the missing females for most of it. Uncle Roderick said you needed us?"

"Yes. Amelia's youngest sister is missing. We aren't sure where she is yet. She recently imprinted on the Duke of Lunsford's son, and it may be something as simple as her sneaking out—or it might be something else. Until we know, the Cavendash's home isn't safe. I need your help to watch over the remaining sisters. Hannah and Poppy are in the drawing room with Mother. Be kind. They are aware of their nature but only recently. They're still a bit stunned and rightly so. Tristan, you go keep them company. The rest of you meet me in the study."

Amelia watched incredulously as they burst into action following Gideon's command.

Gideon waited until they were gone before he turned his attention back to her. "You are free to join us, or you can sit with your sisters, but don't leave the house. Please?"

He was careful not to make his statement a command, and she appreciated his effort.

"I'll go with you."

He grinned. "I hoped you'd say that."

"It's strange. My brothers kept me out of the study most of the time. You're inviting me in."

Gideon brought her hand to his lips and kissed her fingertips. "You are my mate, my most beloved. Anything to do with me concerns you. You deserve to be at my side no matter what. I will never hide anything from you, much less something that involves you. I love you, and I want you with me always."

"Thank you, Gideon, for being exactly what I need. I love you too, more than you can ever imagine."

He dropped a quick kiss on her upturned lips.

"Now, try not to worry. We will do our best to find your sister and the other missing women."

Chapter Nine

Night had fallen far sooner than Amelia would have wished. There had been no word from her family, nor Gideon's father, and though he had sent his cousins out earlier in the day to try and locate them, they had returned unsuccessful by nightfall.

His mother appeared calm on the outside, but she was anxious as well. She wasn't saying anything, but she wasn't her usual chipper self.

Eventually, Amelia sent her sisters to bed, and Gideon sent his cousins to claim the remaining guest rooms. His mother closed herself into her own room, leaving Amelia and Gideon alone.

"You should rest," whispered Gideon.

Amelia had been pacing the hall, occasionally looking out a large window as if she could magically make her sister appear in the streets below.

"I can't. What if they find Lizbeth?"

"I'll wake you."

"You need to sleep too, Gideon."

"I intend to sleep in the same room as you. I assure you, your father will make sure I'm awake when he arrives back. He has no intention of letting me near you until we're wed."

"You put me in your room last night intentionally, didn't you?"

"I've dreamt about you there. I wanted your scent

on my pillows. I knew your father would disapprove, but I also knew he wouldn't let me near you. It was worth it to see you in my—*our* bed."

"I suppose that makes the conjoining bedroom unnecessary doesn't it."

"I can only hope."

Amelia smiled at his agreement and allowed Gideon to lead her into the master bedroom.

"I'll leave the door unlocked so he doesn't think I'm a complete cad. I'd prefer if he forgave me for deflowering you some day."

Her cheeks heated as she imagined that night in her mind.

"I wasn't aware that one innocent touch could make you lose control so easily," she teased softly.

"I didn't think it would either," growled Gideon, and he pulled her toward the bed. "I had just turned twenty, and I thought I had it under control."

"I'm glad you didn't," she admitted.

He grinned. "Me too. I was positively mortified at the time, but it has served me well."

She kissed him on the cheek and turned away from him. "Loosen these ties so I can sleep. I forgot my night rail."

He kissed her exposed shoulder, and his hands went to the ties down the back of her gown. "I can't wait until I can do this every night. You do realize I'm not going to hire you a lady's maid. I consider this to be among my duties as your husband."

She giggled. "You just don't want anyone else to touch me."

"How perceptive of you. I enjoy touching you, and I don't ever want to be robbed of a chance to feel your skin. You're so soft and supple. I'm addicted to this feeling."

Amelia smiled, though he couldn't see. She loved being able to affect him so easily. Since that moment in the garden when she'd asked what he felt like, she hadn't been able to stop. It was as if she was possessed with the need to touch him and be touched by him. The idea that she'd be able to do so whenever she wanted in just a few short weeks made her ridiculously happy. He'd warned her that fateful night that it was a bad idea, and that they shouldn't, but she'd fluttered her eyelashes and he'd given in. She'd been expecting to find a husband soon, despite her earlier rejection of Gideon's initial proposal, and wanted to know what to expect in case the time ever came, but the instant he let her touch him she couldn't or wouldn't consider anyone else. She'd returned the favor and invited him to touch her as well and from then on, they'd been like wildfire, and she didn't regret a single second. She'd looked forward to meeting him as often as possible with more enthusiasm than she'd ever felt. She'd been obsessed, and he'd seemed to feel the same.

"Thus far you've only proven useful in *undressing* me, Gideon. Who will help me put my clothes on if you don't hire a lady's maid?"

He sighed. "I suppose I can become adept at that as well, but it won't be nearly as fun."

"Unless you want the rest of the world to see me naked…"

"I'll just have to fire the staff and dismiss all visitors. We will be true hermits, and I can keep you naked at all times."

Amelia laughed as he finished loosening her gown.

She turned in his arms and smiled up at him. "Your mother expects grandchildren, Gideon. We can't very well raise them while naked. Besides, she will want to spoil them, and she can't do that if you turn her away."

His eyes flashed in surprise. "You intend to have my children?"

"That does usually come after marriage."

"Yes, but I have never heard you say anything like that before."

"We weren't engaged before, but if I became enceinte I was prepared."

"What was your plan?"

"Well, it wouldn't have been difficult to locate you. I would have met you as planned and told you I had missed my courses. As many times as you'd proposed I assumed you would again, probably more insistently, and I would have said yes."

"And now?"

"I don't suppose it will be hard to find you since we'll be married." Amelia chuckled.

He rolled his eyes, and she kicked off her slippers and pulled the pins from her hair.

"What if I hadn't proposed again?"

"My father would have most likely shot you."

He kicked off his shoes, shrugged out of his jacket, and climbed beneath the blankets to lie next to her. He turned on his side and lifted his elbow under his head so he could study her.

"Did you imagine I wouldn't want to have your children?"

He shrugged. "I didn't know if you would after you learned what I am. I was afraid you'd think I was a monster."

She stared up at him and lifted her palm to his cheek. "I've known you far too long to think you're anything other than what you are."

"What am I?"

"You're the only man I've ever considered spending the rest of my life with. You are my heart."

Gideon leaned closer and pressed his forehead against hers. His eyes stayed closed as he spoke. "I still can't resist you," he whispered. He reached between them, grasped her hand, and brought her palm to rest over his heart. "Feel what you do to me."

Amelia sighed blissfully.

"I will always strive to be better for you. You deserve the best of everything I can give you. I will forever be humbled by your love," he vowed softly as he bent to brush his lips across her jaw.

She tilted her head to kiss him briefly on the mouth. "All I want from you is your time and attention. I don't need fancy bobbles or pretty dresses. I don't want anything but these moments with you—that sounds so trite."

"It's perfect," he whispered.

"I just want to be close to you, always."

"I believe we can get much closer," he confessed suggestively. His hand trailed over her hip, and he tugged her body against his, as he continued to press butterfly light kisses to her cheek, throat, and jaw. "How's this?"

"Better," purred Amelia, and she arched up into his grasp. Her hands slipped up beneath his shirt and she pushed it up over his head, revealing a light dusting of dark curls. She raked her fingers through the fine hair across his chest and grinned when he inhaled sharply in response.

"One would think you missed me," teased Gideon. He bunched the material of her skirt in his palm and pulled it up over her hips, exposing her bare skin beneath the blanket.

"I always miss you."

He groaned. "Much as I want this, maybe it isn't the right time…"

"I'm beginning to think there's no such entity as a *right time*. It seems to me that there will always be something we should be more focused on. I believe we should take these moments as they come and appreciate the fact we were granted the opportunity to spend another night together. We might not get another chance. I'm beginning to realize nothing in life is guaranteed."

He gazed down at her thoughtfully as he stroked her skin through the thin material of her undergarments. "As far as inspirational dialogs, that's the most convincing one I've ever heard, but then I think I'm a bit biased. You've always been able to persuade me to your motives."

"It's a gift."

"Then let me make this moment memorable for you—just in case it's our last."

Amelia doubted their time was nearing an end, but life was short, or at least it had been when she'd considered herself human. Shape-shifters seemed to be on an entirely different spectrum, and she had no idea what the rest of her life would look like now that she knew she wasn't like some of the *Ton*. She'd meant what she said, however, and she wasn't going to take any moments spent in her lover's arms for granted.

****

Under most circumstances, Gideon wouldn't have taken advantage of a situation such as this one. He was alone with his mate, and there wasn't a prayer of anyone happening upon them to stop him from having her. It would be the first time in years that he'd had more than a few fleeting minutes alone with Amelia that hadn't been hard earned by sneaking around. He'd been grateful for each and every tryst, but this wasn't a dark nook behind thick curtains where they wouldn't be noticed. This was their home, where they'd be husband and wife—where their children would be born.

His heart thumped heavily with each image his mind conjured. Amelia was in their marital bed, and she was staring up at him as if they were already married. He didn't miss the glaze of desire or how her gaze scoured across his exposed flesh as if she wanted to devour him, and he could think of only one way to pacify the beast that he'd unleashed in her.

His heart raced with anticipation, and he moved his hand closer—between her thighs. "Is this what you wanted?" he asked, his voice far rougher than he meant to sound.

Amelia's reply was a breathy gasp as his fingers made contact with her heated flesh, and she shifted nearer, exposing herself even farther to his explorative touch. "I've always wanted you," she admitted softly, and he watched her eyes close as he stroked her, drawing deep sighs of pleasure from her slightly parted lips.

Gideon watched the emotion play across her face as he pushed her farther and farther toward the unseen edge that would signal her release, and he memorized every detail as if he'd never see it again, storing it away in the deepest recesses of his mind where he kept his most treasured memories. She was beautiful in every way, and she stole the very breath from his lungs. Never in his life would he have imagined that he could have her this way once she knew the truth, and it amazed him that she was still so willing. He supposed it could have something to do with her own recent discovery, but even so, his wildest dreams were coming true, and he wasted no time showing her exactly how he felt about their circumstances.

She writhed against his palm, gasping and moaning as he demonstrated a fraction of his love for her, and in response, he felt her hand slip between them to cup him through his pants, serving only to quicken his pace until she was panting with relief.

He grinned. They'd perfected the ability to pleasure each other as quietly as possible in order to remain secret, and this was no different. The house was full of sleeping wolves with hearing just as superior as his and to some extent Amelia's. Gideon was a selfish man who wanted no one but himself to experience the pure satisfaction of her soft cries of pleasure.

If the moment had ended there, he would've been content to watch her fall asleep fully sated in his arms, but Amelia seemed to be in no hurry to end the night. She reached up and grasped his shoulders, tugging him down on top of her and kissed him hard.

He felt every bit of that kiss, but then she was touching him again, and he forgot that he'd meant to make *her* night memorable. Breeches and other small clothes were quickly dispensed with. His breath caught in his chest when she guided him toward her. He obliged her seductive and unspoken plea—burying himself inside Amelia until everything seemed right with the world once more.

The alpha in him demanded satisfaction, but Gideon forced himself to keep a rigid control. This was about her. He needed her to understand how much he loved her, because what he had planned next could destroy everything.

****

Edgar Cowen snarled viciously as his gaze darted around the crumbling shack of a house. He smashed his fist into the wall, only briefly satisfied when it began to crumble under his brute strength.

"You brought the wrong girl!" He spun to face the cowering rogues under his control and glowered at them. "Featherbrains!" His temper raged, and he stalked toward the trio of rogues he'd sent to fetch Amelia, while the three others he'd managed to find only that morning stood unaffected by his rage near the door.

"You said—" began one of the rogues timidly, the only one that was even remotely in control of his blood lust.

Edgar roared. "You're all useless!"

The females he'd captured huddled together, with their new addition, the younger sister of his intended bride. She sobbed into one of the other women's arms, but Edgar didn't feel an ounce of remorse. His fury only rose as he stared at her.

"You had *one* task! One! She doesn't even look like the female I told you to grab!" His fists clenched, and he stomped toward the rogue closest to him.

The man whimpered like a kicked dog, and Edgar

gloried in the stench of the other man's fear as he latched onto his throat and lifted him into the air. Blood coated his fingers as he sank his nails into the man's skin, tearing his life away from him. He stared into his victim's eyes, and the life fading from his terrified gaze gave Edgar relief, until finally the man's body went slack and Edgar was no longer satisfied. He threw the man's lifeless body across the room, startling the three women into a cacophony of desperate caterwauling.

He turned on the remaining two rogues. "You will take these females and meet me in Glasgow. I don't think I need to warn you of what will happen if you disappoint me again."

He glanced at the three newest members of his pack. "You three will come with me."

He was quickly running out of rogues to command, no thanks to London's alpha, and Edgar couldn't afford to lose another. This could be his last chance to take his mate and make her his own.

Chapter Ten

The next morning Amelia entered the drawing room to find Gideon's mother was no longer making an effort to hide her anxiety. She sat in a corner of the drawing room knitting furiously as if the hounds of hell were on her tail.

Hannah sat in the opposite corner with a stack of books, and Poppy occupied herself by chatting with Tristan—which did not bode well at all. Gideon's cousin appeared enamored with her younger sister, and Amelia had to fight the urge to separate them—especially after Tristan admitted that he thought Poppy was his mate.

Gideon kept a calm demeanor, but Amelia could feel his concern. His father should have been back by now. As should her parents and the rest of the party searching for her sister.

"They've never been apart this long," he whispered. Both he and Amelia were standing in the study across the hall, with the doors to both rooms open so that they could all see one another, but far enough away that no one should be able to hear what she and Gideon discussed.

"But he's fine or wouldn't she…" Amelia couldn't finish her thought.

"I see my mother has been educating you," he spoke through clenched teeth. "I had hoped she wouldn't mention certain facts."

"Like how you could become a rogue if I had died without letting you mark me? Or how you could die if I was killed after we're mated?" She stared up at him pointedly

"I could care less what happens to me. You are the one I need to be careful with. After you accept my mark, I will take every precaution with my own life to make sure you are safe."

"You could have become a rogue, Gideon," she growled.

He sighed and rested his forehead against hers. He didn't say anything—instead he turned his head slightly and nuzzled her cheek against his.

Despite her displeasure, she melted into his arms— her entire body alive with a slow burn of pleasure. It wasn't intense like the forest fire that engulfed them when he ran his hands along her curves. This was a smoldering heat that promised an explosion if she didn't contain the flame. She looked forward to exploring that option later, but for now she was content to feel the heat.

"How long are we going to wait for their return before we go out looking for them?"

"I can't let you go out there, Amelia. It's not safe."

"You can't make me stay either, Gideon."

"If you go, your sisters will too. You are their leader right now. You have to keep them safe."

"Actually, I only have to worry about Hannah. Your cousin seems to have Poppy under control."

"Amelia—"

"I'm not letting you go without me, Gideon. I waited too long to hear you say you love me. I'm not giving you up now when we're so close to being together in all the ways I've ever dreamt of."

His grip tightened. "I have no willpower when it comes to you."

"Then what are we going to do?"

"We'll wait until tomorrow morning. If they haven't returned, I'll call for reinforcements. Lord Covington will be willing to help since his daughter is your brother's mate. We'll expand our search. I'll also check in with Lord Lunsford. His pack will be willing to help as well since it concerns Lizbeth. I have a few other connections we'll exhaust, after that…"

"What more can we do?"

"I'm the alpha of my pack. I can't just abandon the ones I have here to search for those missing, not without leaving a second in my place. If I have to, I'll leave Tristan in charge as a last resort. But if we leave, my mother will not stay behind either. I guarantee it. Are you willing to leave your sister in my cousin's care, possibly permanently if we don't return?"

"They need to be protected." Amelia nodded. "If it's what's best."

"Tristan is the next in line to lead my pack should something happen to my father or me."

"Do you trust him?"

"Yes."

"Then so do I."

As the hours flowed by, no one wanted to acknowledge the obvious. Gideon sent for his friends, and the other alphas in London loaned their men out to search, but everyone remained silent. His mother had withdrawn completely. Her skin now waxed pale as a new moon. She had retired early rather than face the rest of them. Hannah had gone to bed as well with another book to occupy her mind, and Poppy was still sitting far closer to Tristan than was appropriate. It was a complete disaster. But eventually Amelia coaxed her younger sister to retire as well. Now she and Gideon could get the sleep they needed before leaving in the morning.

****

Gideon snuck out like a thief in the night, his mind weighted with guilt and knowing full well what would happen as a result. Amelia would be angry, most likely she'd call off the wedding, and he didn't blame her. He'd let her believe she would be accompanying him when they set out to find her sister, but he couldn't. He wouldn't put her in danger.

As a female, a half-blooded Omega no less, who'd never completely shifted, Amelia was too vulnerable. The rogues would kill her, and he would never be able to function without her. His heart nearly beat out of his chest at the mere thought. He refused to think of her in danger, and as she'd lain sleeping next to him, he kissed her cheek and softly bid her goodbye.

Gideon had snatched his coat and boots and slipped out of his own room as if he'd stolen something, and headed for the door, where he unintentionally met his mother in the upstairs hallway. She looked frail but appeared well for the moment. She needed her mate, and Gideon needed to bring his family home, even if his betrayal meant Amelia never spoke to him again.

His mother smiled at him and bowed her head in acknowledgement. She had to know what he was doing, but she didn't try to stop him. The sun would be rising soon, and he needed to leave before Amelia awoke.

Without a word, he kissed his mother's cheek in farewell and continued down the hall until he found the room where his cousin Tristan should be sleeping. He knocked once, rousing the male from his bed, and announced that he was leaving, and that Amelia would be in charge until he returned. But a woman in charge could be taken advantage of, and he knew Tristan would not behave in such a way.

He forced his cousin to swear to protect her, and then left to join the other alphas waiting for him near the edge of London.

After Amelia had gone to bed last night, Gideon had met with his scouts to discuss the plans for the following morning. He'd been relieved to find they'd picked up the rogues' scent near the Thames, where Gideon himself had done the same only days earlier. The ball that should've announced his engagement seemed like so long ago that Gideon had nearly forgotten that he'd sent his men to search the area.

Thankfully, his intuition had proven true, and his men returned with a glimmer of hope.

They'd found the house where the rogues had been hiding out, and they'd scented the missing girls as well, but they'd been too late. The group had already moved on. Their tracks were still fresh, however, and Gideon knew he couldn't waste another second waiting for his father to return—he had to go after the rogues now.

It appeared the rogues and their hostages headed out of London toward their destination—which appeared to be Glasgow—so Gideon ordered his search party to meet him just inside his territory, so they could leave as one. Once they passed through the forest line surrounding London, they would no longer be within his jurisdiction. Outside his boundaries the rogues would consider it to be no man—*or wolf's* land. With no rules to govern them once they left London, it was every beast for himself.

Gideon was determined to bring the girls—and hopefully his family back, because there was no way he could go home and face his mate, nor his mother without them.

Chapter Eleven

Amelia awoke expecting to find Gideon lying next to her, but he was nowhere to be found. His shoes were gone, as well as his jacket, and her heart sank. Quickly, she slipped into her slippers and tightened the front ties of her bodice, uncaring that the top button on the back of her dress was likely still undone as she rushed downstairs and into the dining room. Lady Rochester sat silently picking at the food on her plate, while Hannah munched absently. Poppy giggled at something Tristan said, but Gideon was not present.

Her heart hammered wildly, and she struggled to catch her breath. "Where's Gideon?" She tried to hide the sound of her panic, but she knew it was evident in her voice.

When neither Tristan nor Gideon's mother would meet her gaze, her heart sank. They didn't need to say it out loud—she could feel his absence in the pits of her soul. Gideon had abandoned her to search on his own.

"He left early this morning, and he said you're in charge for a while," explained Tristan, his voice carefully devoid of emotion.

"Excuse me?" Gideon's mother gasped. "Are you saying Gideon left? As in, he left *London*? I believed he was merely continuing his search within our boundaries." Her protest sounded hollow to Amelia.

"He wanted to get an early start. He and the Duke

of Covington set out four hours ago."

He was dead. Amelia clenched her jaw. She was going to *kill* him when he returned, and he had better return because if he didn't, she was going to find a witch to resurrect him and kill him again! Because if shape-shifters existed, then witches surely did too.

"He didn't tell you he was leaving?" queried Gideon's mother, turning toward Amelia.

"Of course not! Do you think I would have let him go without me? He's hardly traveled more than a few miles away since we met. Why would I allow him to go looking for my sister without me? This was not our plan!"

"Surely, he mentioned something to you—he's been stalking you for years. He wouldn't just leave you," insisted Gideon's mother.

Amelia glared at the floor. "Yes, he would—if he thought it was too dangerous. And he hasn't been *stalking* me, he's been *hunting* me. He also knows I won't leave my sisters to go after him. That's why he told me to trust Tristan. He planned to leave me here all along."

"But he can't lie to you—you're his mate," asserted his mother.

"He didn't lie to me, he said *we*, he never said he and I. When he said *we* he meant he and the other alphas. This was his plan all along!"

"Forgive me," began Poppy. "I have been educating myself on the ways of shifters, and you're an Omega. You can't be an alpha, so who's *really* in charge?"

"Unofficially I am, but Gideon said specifically that *she* was, so unless he dies, Amelia is the leader for now," admitted Tristan reluctantly.

"I'm pretty sure Amelia is the least qualified to lead us," huffed Hannah.

"I beg your pardon?" Amelia gasped indignantly.

Hannah shrugged. "You have broken every law of decorum that mother ever set for us. You've been sneaking out to meet Gideon since you turned eighteen, you avoid all the most prestigious events, and you never listen to Parker or father. You raise your voice, and you argue with everyone—forgive me but it sounds to me as if you're the one who needs to be led."

"No, no, dear. Those are the rules among the *Ton*. But you girls are not fully human. You're part wolves, and *that* is precisely the type of leader we need. People who question the laws and fight for our rights. Amelia is a perfect leader for us, but Poppy is right. She's an Omega, so she can't be a permanent leader. The pack will listen to her for a bit because Gideon is a good leader, and also out of respect for his command, but just as an Omega does not bend to alpha decrees, the pack does not submit to hers. They'll listen until they think Gideon isn't coming back, and then Tristan will have to take over," explained Gideon's mother.

"Then let's hope for all our sakes that Gideon comes back because I do not want to be mated to the alpha of London," admitted Poppy.

"And I don't want to *be* the alpha of London," agreed Tristan.

"Gideon said London was neutral territory," began Amelia, a feeling of betrayal settling in her stomach.

"Oh, it is—because Gideon said so. All the alphas who live here have his permission," announced Gideon's mother.

"He lied to me."

"Not exactly," said his mother.

"I trusted him, and he deceived me! Twice," she snarled. "Were you in on this? All those things you said, was it just to get me to trust him?"

"Now see here," began Lady Rochester as she rose angrily from her chair.

"Did you mean anything you said?"

"Of course! You are my son's mate—you might as well be my own daughter."

"Yes, but was it because I am supposed to be the alpha's mate or because you wanted my favor? Has everyone lost their minds? Has the last fourteen years of my life been little more than a game for your family?"

"How dare—"

"How dare *you*," Amelia protested. "How dare you manipulate me! I am not a chess piece to be maneuvered wherever you see fit. I was a child!"

"You can't just—"

"*Yes, I can!*"

Tristan stood as if to defend his aunt.

"SIT DOWN!"

Slowly he lowered back into his seat, eyes wide. "I thought you said she's an Omega," he hissed.

Lady Rochester studied her. "Gideon didn't bite you. So you shouldn't be able to unlock your wolf if you're not an Omega."

"Does it matter? I am a person. I have feelings. I don't deserve to be treated like an object!"

"Amelia, I have never once lied to you. Since the moment I met you, since Gideon connected with you, I have looked after you, cared for you, trusted you with

155

my son. I did not manipulate you. This is how shifter politics are. I don't know why Gideon didn't tell you the truth, but I had nothing to do with that. *Of course*, I want you to trust my son—you're his mate. I want him to be happy. I could care less about your favor other than as your future mother-in-law and the grandmother of your children!"

Amelia clenched her fists. She didn't know what or who to believe anymore.

A knock sounded at the door, interrupting her thoughts, and she watched in frustration as Gideon's mother raced away, giving the footman no time to respond.

"It might be Lizbeth," whispered Poppy hopefully.

"Or Papa," agreed Hannah.

Amelia turned her attention back toward the entry where Lady Rochester was literally backing into the room. Lord Cowen almost pushing her over in his haste to gain access to the dining room.

"Did Gideon send you," demanded Amelia, not caring one bit how rude she must sound.

"I'm here for you," announced Lord Cowen.

He wasn't lying, but neither was he telling the truth, and she could sense the reluctance in his tone.

"To help?" asked Tristan, and he took a step forward, putting himself between Lord Cowen and Amelia's sisters.

Gideon's mother continued to falter toward the group and away from the uninvited guest as if his presence repulsed her.

"If Gideon sent you, that means you're one of us—right?" asked Amelia, unsure.

Tristan scoffed. "He's a wolf, but he's hardly one

of us."

"But I've seen him on different occasions. Why would Gideon invite him if he isn't part of the pack," demanded Poppy.

"To not invite him to a pack event would give Lord Cowen the right to challenge Gideon's role as our leader. It's better to extend an invitation out of duty than to snub him and risk upsetting the pack dynamics," explained Tristan, his gaze still glued to the unexpected visitor.

"Like we do with Lady Walch," muttered Hannah darkly.

Amelia crossed her arms in defense as Lord Cowen, a middle age man with sallow skin and red-rimmed eyes drew even closer. "That's close enough, thank you. We have it under control here, so you can leave until Gideon returns." She leveled a warning gaze on the intruder, hoping he'd fall under her command the same way Tristan had, but he didn't seem affected.

"Your worthless mate has abandoned you, Amelia—and for what? A few alphas and some light skirts?" Lord Cowen snorted. "He doesn't deserve your admiration."

Amelia's hackles rose. "You have no right to speak of my betrothed that way, how dare you! Get out! Now!"

"No, I don't think so. You see, Gideon is exactly where I want him to be at this moment, and I can't waste any more time waiting for you to come to your senses. You're coming with me. We can do this the hard way, or the easy way." He grinned maliciously. "I much prefer the hard way."

Her skin crawled and she took a shocked step back

toward Tristan. "I hardly even know you!"

"But I know you, Amelia. I know *everything* about you—who your parents are, where you came from, what you are. Come with me and I'll tell you anything you want to know."

Amelia scowled. "I already know all those things, my parents—"

"Lied to you! You're not Henry's daughter. But I know who your real parents are. I know how you came to be a ward of Henry and Marian Cavendash, and I know how you can find your brother."

Amelia stared in shocked dismay at the Duke of Edington. He wasn't lying. As a wolf shifter, Amelia would've known, she would've heard the increase in his heart rate if he'd been fabricating his tale, but there was no tell-tale sign of a falsehood. Every word out of his mouth seemed absolutely and appallingly true!

"Don't listen to him, Amelia. You're our sister, you *know* that," insisted Poppy.

But Amelia couldn't hear past the roaring in her ears. Lord Cowen *wasn't* lying. She knew it as surely as she knew her own name.

"Get out," snapped Tristan furiously. "You have no right to be here or to say such blasphemous things. Leave!"

Lord Cowen smirked. "But I'm not lying, am I, Amelia?"

Amelia swallowed, and her hands trembled as she raised them to hug herself in a vain attempt at comfort.

Their undesirable guest cocked his head to one side as if he heard something they didn't. "Not yet!" He twisted to face the hallway where three men stood. Lord Cowen turned once more to face Amelia. "Apparently we're doing this the easy way—pity."

Amelia gasped in fear as one by one the men dropped to their hands and knees. With a blur of flesh and fur they changed into some of the largest wolves she'd ever seen and began to stalk around Lord Cowen. The putrid scent of rotting flesh and drying blood filled the air as they drew closer.

"Hannah, Poppy, run," cried Amelia in terror, her gaze on the Duke.

She heard her sisters flee, and out the corner of her eye, she watched in horror as one of the wolves went after them. A fourth wolf jumped into his path, and Amelia knew immediately the large dark-colored wolf with doe brown eyes was Tristan.

A fifth wolf, somewhat smaller, stalked up beside Amelia and snarled at the remaining two wolves.

As one, the rogues lunged at Lady Rochester. Amelia barely managed to leap out of the way in time to avoid colliding with them.

The third wolf who had gone after her sisters broke off his pursuit, and headed back toward Amelia, his head bent low, snarling and growling as he crept toward her. She watched him crouch as he prepared to leap, and something inside of her snapped.

This was the last straw. It was one thing for her family to lie to her and hide things, it was even worse for her mate, whom she trusted above all else, to dupe her. Now she was being hunted by the very things that had stolen her sister and killed countless other young girls. This was going to end *today*!

Amelia's spine bent. The pain so excruciating she dropped to her hands and knees. She had no idea what was happening. Her entire body ached and burned, and her fists curved viciously against the tile. A snarl ripped from her throat, and she bared her teeth. Her head spun, an instant of disorientation, and suddenly everything became crystal clear. At the end of her face, she glimpsed a long white snout and fur as pristine as new fallen snow. She could see everything with an intense clarity, and her sense of smell was heightened. Her brain catalogued it all with blinding speed. She wasn't naked as she'd presumed she might be, in the event of a change, and her clothes weren't lying in tattered pieces around her feet as she'd originally suspected but had disappeared along with her human body. Leaving behind the wolf, a vaguely familiar entity that had claimed residence in her mind but was now a physical individual, with strength and power radiating from her core.

Her would-be attacker hesitated as if he hadn't been expecting her to change, and she utilized his distraction to leap. She had no idea how she knew what to do, but it was as if her body knew how to bend, how to land, where to sink her teeth, and where to shove her back paws.

Razor sharp claws sliced into the rogue's gut. Her fangs sank deep into his throat until she tasted blood on her tongue. She clamped down and didn't let go, until he stopped convulsing.

Satisfied, she released the wolf's body and turned her attention toward Lady Rochester. How dare this rogue think to attack a member of *her* pack?

"Amelia, stop!" Lord Cowen attempted to cut her off.

Amelia didn't hesitate. Her fury rose, and she stalked toward the remaining wolf. She pounced on his back just as he tossed the smaller wolf across the room.

The rogue wolf yelped in shock when Amelia landed on his spine, and her fangs bit deep into his scruff. Her hind legs kicked at his backside, leaving deep bloody grooves along the base of his tail. He tried to shake her off, but she held on and jerked her head from side to side until he too collapsed and remained motionless.

She left him and prepared to tackle the third and final rogue when she realized Tristan had already taken care of him. Satisfied that the rogues were no longer a threat, Amelia spun to face their final contender.

"Now, Amelia, wait just one second…I'm the only one who knows the truth." Lord Cowen seemed to shrink under Amelia's scornful gaze, as if he couldn't quite believe what he was seeing.

Amelia didn't answer, she couldn't. In her wolf form, she took a threatening step toward the duke, and he quickly took several more back away from her and threw up his hands in defense.

"Amelia, listen to me, I *know* everything. I know who you are. You don't belong here." He sounded uncertain as he struggled to bring her back under control.

She stalked closer, and bared her fangs, daring him to utter another word. She desperately wanted to find out what he could possibly know about her, but she couldn't persuade her wolf to stand down.

"Amelia, I can get Lizbeth back."

She recognized his words as a last-ditch attempt for what it was. Amelia tried to leash her inner beast in an effort to regain control, but her she-wolf insisted that if he could get Lizbeth back, then he was clearly the one who'd taken her. This only fueled the wolf's fury and caused her to pull harder. Amelia struggled to keep a grip on herself, but the wolf was so strong, and she felt herself creeping even closer toward Lord Cowen.

"Blasted wench!" Lord Cowen swore and raced toward the door, scurrying off into the street like a screeching rat.

Amelia's wolf insisted they go after him, but suddenly her exertion of power began to fade, and Amelia found herself far too exhausted to do much more than collapse. Relieved that he was finally gone, she dropped to her belly, lay on her side, and without any prompting on her part she felt the brief disorientation that signaled the change, leaving her once more a fully clothed lady.

****

Gideon was miles outside of Glasgow, a trip that *should have* taken more than ten hours—but his paws burned up the distance as he and the other wolves ran in wolf form, tracking the scent of the rogues and the missing females.

His heart raced, his mind spinning a mile a minute as he considered the duplicity he'd dealt his mate.

Amelia would hate him. She would never speak to him again. He'd most likely have to challenge her wolf just to be able to get close to her, but it would be worth a few cuts or bites. He'd do anything it took to have her in any possible way he could.

He prayed her pack would convince her to forgive him, but he didn't hold out much hope for absolution. Amelia had a temper as hot as any she-wolf, and he knew she'd retaliate in one way or another, especially now that she understood her effect on him. He was in for a long, miserable life, but for him there hadn't been any other choice. His pack depended on him. *Her* pack depended on him. It was his duty as the alpha of London to protect the wolves who chose to make their homes there, and if she couldn't see that...he'd spend the rest of his life trying to convince her.

Gideon sped through the countryside at a blinding speed far faster than any horse. There was no doubt in his mind that he'd make it to the port city within the hour if he didn't stop for a break.

As predicted, Gideon and those he traveled with arrived in Glasgow just as the noon sun hit its zenith. They'd all shifted back to human form and were prepared to infiltrate the city when he caught the familiar scent of his father and the others who'd gone to search for Lizbeth as well as the rogues. He followed their scents to a small tavern just outside the city and stomped inside, prepared to defend his pack.

However, there were no rogues. Instead, Gideon found the rest of his missing pack sitting in the drawing room of the tavern, and in their midst were Lizbeth and the missing girls, who were all crying hysterically. Presumably the reason they had not yet started back toward London.

"What happened?" he demanded breathlessly.

His father stood. "We tracked the rogues to just outside Glasgow and took care of them. What are you doing here? Who's looking after the rest of the pack?"

"Tristan and Amelia."

Lord Cavendash cursed. "You were supposed to keep my girls safe, Gideon!"

"I am. More than half of my cousins are in London. A couple of them are at or near my townhouse. Only an *imbecile* would attack them now."

"We spoke to a couple of the rogues—while they still lived. The group was much larger than we originally imagined," asserted Lord Cavendash. "And they weren't after Lizbeth. They were trying to get to Amelia."

Gideon felt his heart drop. "No…that's impossible—they're not capable of logic—they can't plan something like that."

"The two we talked with weren't as far gone with madness as the others. They admitted it was a mistake. He said they were ordered to kidnap Amelia, but they took the wrong girl. They wanted her for a mate." Lord Cavendash cleared his throat anxiously. "You should go back to London, Gideon. We'll get the girls back safely."

Gideon snarled and barreled out of the room without another coherent word. His instincts were on high as he smashed into the forest and forced himself to change into his wolf faster than he'd ever shifted before. *No one* was going to touch his mate. His heart stuttered in rage as he took off flying across the country once more. He would stop for nothing until his mate was safe.

Chapter Twelve

"Amelia?"

The sound of her name beat like a hammer against her temple. Amelia groaned, clutched her head, and forced her eyes open.

Lady Rochester stood over her, fanning her, while both Hannah and Poppy sat on the floor next to her.

Poppy offered her a glass of water, and Amelia gulped it down.

"Let me help you," urged Hannah, when Amelia attempted to sit up.

For a moment her head swam, and she thought she would retch, but then the world balanced out once more and the urge passed.

"You blacked out, dear one. You've been unconscious for hours. Are you all right?" asked Lady Rochester softly.

"I think so." They helped her to her feet, and Amelia stood unsteadily.

"An Omega should not be able to take out a rogue, much less two, Aunt Gertie," hissed Tristan. He was standing a little away from Amelia, studying her as if she'd grown a second head.

"I know, dear," began Gideon's mother, as if she wasn't quite ready to discuss what had happened.

Amelia glanced around the room, unsure if she'd really killed some of the rogues or if she'd simply imagined it happened. It was night now, but it seemed like only minutes since she'd awakened to find her mate missing.

Blood stained the floor in several places. The rogues' bodies, still in wolf form, lay scattered about exactly as she and Tristan had left them. She assumed because he didn't want to leave the house without having another male to stand guard.

The entry door thumped open, and Amelia immediately panicked, until she looked up to see Gideon. His chest moved up and down rapidly, as his brown-eyed gaze circled the room.

"Tristan?" asked Gideon, who looked at his cousin. "You took the rogues out all on your own?"

Tristan coughed somewhat in embarrassment. "Not me, cousin." He pointed at Amelia. "I had help."

Gideon took a step toward his mate, and Amelia snarled in response.

"Don't touch me," she snapped viciously. "Don't ever touch me." She held up her hands defensively and backed away.

"It's all right, my love, you did well," he began encouragingly.

More footsteps sounded, as the rest of her missing friends and family entered the room, just a few minutes behind Gideon.

"You lied to me! You *all* lied to me." She growled low as her mind threatened to overwhelm her.

"Now, Amelia," began her father defensively.

"You especially, *Father*."

"What is she talking about?" whispered Lizbeth breathlessly in confusion.

"She's not an Omega, Gideon," announced Tristan.

"She doesn't even have the right color fur of any shifter I have ever seen."

"Don't talk about me like I'm not here," insisted Amelia, her voice raspy with rage.

Tristan immediately swallowed and backed across the room as if she might go after him next. He sat near Poppy, and her father immediately started to intervene.

"No!" Amelia held her hand up to stop her father. "You don't get to decide for her."

"What has gotten into you?" demanded Parker.

"I know what this is about," admitted their father softly.

Lord Rochester sighed. "You knew it would come out eventually."

Her mother swallowed hard. "Amelia, we need to talk—"

"Why? So you can keep lying to me? I don't care what you have to say. I don't care what any of you say. You treated me like I was addlepated. You made me feel like I was less than you, like I didn't deserve to know what was happening to me. All this time you knew, and you didn't tell me. I trusted you, *all* of you!" She scowled at Gideon then. "You tricked me. I trusted you more than anyone, and you manipulated me!" She took another step back as Gideon attempted to touch her once more. "No, you don't get to touch me. I hate you. I hate all of you!" She shuddered shamefully as the words left her mouth, knowing full well that she didn't mean any of it. However, she was too hurt and dazed by the events of the day to take back her words.

"I want to come with you, Amelia," whispered Poppy as Amelia started to head for the door.

"Poppy." Their father gasped in shock.

167

Poppy sighed sadly. "You're my father, and I love you, but I don't want an alpha I can't trust."

"Lud, Poppy," hissed Parker in stunned disbelief.

"You didn't think twice before running off after Lizbeth. You left us here and assumed Amelia would watch after us, and you were right. She did. I trust her. If I have to be a wolf and have a leader, then I choose her. Tristan said I would be able to choose who my alpha is if I'm an Omega, and I choose her. I'm sorry. I love you."

"She's right," decided Hannah timidly. "I'm going with Amelia too."

"You are *women*, you won't survive without an alpha," sneered Lord Lunsford.

"I AM AN ALPHA!"

Lord Lunsford—a formidable alpha in his own right, paled at the authority in Amelia's voice.

"Please…hear us out," whispered Amelia's mother gravely. "You have every right to feel betrayed, but you deserve to know the truth."

Amelia didn't want to hear anything they had to say, but because it was her mother she agreed warily.

"Fine." She took a seat at the dining table and watched stiffly as the others took seats on the other side, leaving Poppy and Hannah to sit next to Amelia.

"Your parents, your *birth* parents…" began her mother softly.

"No…wait…" Amelia felt her stomach plummet. *It was all true. What Lord Cowen had told her earlier. She'd hoped he was wrong.*

"You have to listen," pleaded Lord Cavendash.

Amelia shook her head desperately.

"You're right. We have lied to you your entire life.

You are not a half-blood—you're my niece. My brother's daughter. My family comes from a long line of full-blooded alphas—in fact, my brother and I were twins. As the oldest he should have been the Duke, but he didn't want the title. He didn't want anything to do with the *Ton* and human people. I took his place, with Rochester's help, and my brother left. He met his mate some time later. She was from Greenland. She had white-blonde hair and green eyes, and the whitest fur we'd ever seen. You favor your birth mother in every way. Her family were from a rare blood line that produced only white wolves. But you didn't carry the wolf scent and I thought…maybe it had skipped you. It's happened before."

Amelia couldn't stop the tears from flowing. "I don't want to hear any more," she whispered brokenly.

"They died shortly after you were born," continued Marian Cavendash sympathetically.

Amelia stared at the woman who'd always been her mother, and for the first time in her life she only saw a stranger. Her entire existence had been nothing but a lie. She wasn't their daughter.

"Your mother's pack kept your twin brother."

Amelia shook her head. "Stop."

"You were just a baby, and we have loved you as our own," insisted Amelia's mother.

"Enough!" Amelia stood to leave and swiped at her tears angrily. "I don't want to know any more."

"Amelia—"

She shook her head. "You knew what I was all this time, and you kept it from me. You taught the boys, but you didn't teach *me*, even though you knew I might change whether I had a mate or not! I'm a full-blood like you, but you didn't want me to know. Why?"

"Because…" Her father sighed. "It was too dangerous. Your father made me promise to keep you safe."

Amelia hesitated. "You could've told me I was a shape-shifter without telling me who my parents were—why couldn't you tell me the truth?"

"Your parents were murdered by rogues. They fought to stay alive just long enough to see you and your brother safe, and they begged us not to tell you about him. They were afraid the rogues would hunt you down if you ever tried to go home. I was afraid you'd try anyway if we told you the truth. You would've asked questions, and I couldn't have lied to you. You were already so interested in our world. It was easier to have you believe otherwise. You're stubborn, just like your father," confessed Henry Cavendash roughly. "Then Gideon came around, and we realized he was your mate. You couldn't leave him, or you would have died. Mates can't be apart for more than a few weeks, even as children. That's why we brought Lizbeth to London. We were just trying to protect you. You would've found out eventually. We just thought if you didn't learn the whole truth, you would stay with us where you would be safe. You're our daughter, we just wanted—"

"No, I'm not." Amelia scowled. "I'm not your daughter." She backed away from the table. "I was *supposed* to be the Duke of Cavendash's daughter but I'm not. I'm the Duke's *niece*."

Hannah and Poppy rose as if to follow, and Amelia held up her hand.

"Stay. Stay with Parker." She glanced at the man

she'd thought was her eldest brother but didn't say a word to acknowledge him.

Gideon rose as well, and she gave a warning growl. "You stay away from me."

"Growl all you want, Amelia, but you know I'm not going to let you leave by yourself."

She glared at him and continued out the door. Although he followed her, at least Gideon had the good sense not to say a word.

****

Gideon could practically feel his heart being ripped from his chest. Never in his life had anything hurt as much as his mate's rejection. He'd tried to prepare himself for her wrath, but he'd never thought she'd react so strongly. Not to push him away.

His beloved's despair and emotional upheaval had him wanting to go to her and comfort her, but it would be a mistake to touch Amelia. Not right now, not when his betrayal cut so deep.

Her sobs were soul-wrenching to hear, and his heart broke for her. They weren't mated yet, but he could feel her emotions as if he had a direct line to her heart. It was the damnedest thing, but he welcomed it over the alternative. Without the bond, he'd feel nothing—would have no clue how she felt, and his beast would rage, bringing him ever closer to going rogue. He'd spent years trying to earn her trust, and it had all been ripped away in an instant. His one glimmer of hope was the fact that he still felt her. Despite what she claimed, she still loved him.

He trailed behind her when she left his home, uncaring that she snarled at him like a wild animal and demanded he leave her alone. He couldn't. He *wouldn't*. He'd spent his entire day in wolf form, pushing his body beyond its limits, and all he wanted was to collapse in her arms and sleep for a week. Gideon had been terrified of losing her to death, and his run across the country was fueled completely by desperation. He'd arrived back at the house in human form, scented the rogues, and nearly exposed himself to anyone on the street by shifting back into his wolf right then and there. He hadn't cared if the good people of London saw him change from human to beast. In that moment nothing else had mattered. It had taken him precious seconds to realize it wasn't her blood he smelled, and he managed to pull himself under control at the very last instant.

He'd walked into his own house praying to every deity he'd ever heard of that she would be unharmed and nearly dissolved into tears of relief when he found her safe. In that moment, it hadn't mattered that she'd looked at him as if he'd betrayed her. For one second, he was too glad she was alive to care that she hated him. But as the high of relief and adrenaline finally left him, her pain came racing in to replace his own, and his heart plunged once more. She despised him. She would likely never willingly speak to him again.

Amelia didn't appear to know where she was going, nor did she seem to care. She lowered her head, avoiding the curious stares of her peers, and headed down the streets of London past her family's townhouse—toward the cemetery.

She proceeded through the tall iron gates and passed tomb after tomb after tomb. Amelia kept walking until the graves became crumbling reminders of people who'd perished long before Gideon's birth.

She careened through the graveyard until the grass became unkempt, and still she stumbled on. At last she stopped beneath a wide willow tree. The heavy vine-like branches drooped, swaying softly—welcoming them, and she dropped to her hands and knees beneath its canopy. The exact spot where they normally met in secret. He wasn't certain if she'd realized where she'd run to, or if it even mattered to Amelia that she'd come to the exact place they'd always found a way to be together in, but it mattered to him.

Even in anger, she still sought reminders of their stolen moments together, and he hoped from the deepest regions of his heart that it meant she still wanted him. If she gave up on their relationship, he'd never be able to help her heal from her family's deception, and if nothing else, he wanted her to be happy, even if it meant without him.

"Amelia." He said her name softly, but she didn't respond.

Chapter Thirteen

"Amelia."

"Don't touch me," she mumbled miserably. Her heart ached so much, she feared it would shatter. Her fingers sought and grasped threads of grass in an effort to anchor herself.

The ground vibrated when Gideon dropped down beside her, and then his arm draped around her back, and he pulled her toward him.

Amelia hesitated momentarily but eventually allowed him to pull her into his arms. There she fell apart in complete despair and cried as if a dam had burst, until every last tear left her body. Still, she didn't move—she couldn't. Her entire world had been ripped out from under her and left her broken with no hope of ever recovering.

The sun was rising when she finally stirred. Gideon hadn't let her go the entire time, and she was grateful. As much as she wanted to hate him, she couldn't.

"You tricked me," she accused hoarsely, her voice rough and uneven.

"I know."

"I trusted you."

"I know."

"You told me London was neutral. Why did you lie?"

"I didn't lie. London *is* neutral. I didn't tell you

that it was my territory because I didn't want you to be lured by the title. I wanted you to love me for me. I wanted London to be different than everywhere else. The territory has been in my family for generations— it's one of the most populated cities for miles. Finding a mate is already one of the most difficult things a wolf— or anyone—ever has to accomplish, and creatures were constantly trying to sneak in for a chance to find their beloved mates. There was a time when a creature could be killed just for being on another's territory without permission. I didn't like that, I wanted peace, and when my father stepped down as alpha, I took it as an opportunity to make London available for everyone.

"The more people who find their mates, means less rogues we have to deal with. I allowed everyone to make their home here in hopes that it could make things better for our people, and as a result, the people who reside here are under my protection. I told you each family was their own pack, and that's not a lie. When those who choose to leave London, they are no longer part of our pack, but while they're here I am their alpha. As far as I'm aware, no one else does this, but I didn't tell you, because I didn't want you to see me as anything more than just a man in love with you."

"But you know me," she murmured. "You know I'm not that way."

He sighed. "I had to be sure."

"You left me."

"I couldn't risk you, Amelia. You're too important to me."

"But you made me think we were going together."

"You wouldn't have stayed if I'd told you the truth. I'm sorry I didn't tell you, but I don't regret leaving you behind. You are my entire world—the reason I get up each morning. If something happened to you—" He swallowed. "—I won't make it without you. I don't want to. I need you in my life. Without you, I don't exist. You can be angry all you want, but I am always going to protect you."

Amelia wanted to continue detesting his very existence—wanted to hold on to her anger, but everything he said made too much sense. She could feel his sincerity and knew if it had been up to her she would have done the same thing. Gideon was one of the most important people in her entire life, and if she lost him… Her heart throbbed painfully. She didn't want to think about what that would mean.

"I don't know who I am anymore."

"You are nothing less than you've always been," he reminded her. "You're still you, and I have had the honor of knowing exactly who you are from the moment I met you, because you are the most honest, amazing woman I've ever met. All my most favorite memories are with you, and none of that will ever change. You are still Amelia Cavendash—my mate, my betrothed, my love, and the future mother of my children. You are still the most beautiful, kind, caring, and brave, love of my life. You are you, and that's all you will ever need to be. Nothing about who you are changes just because things didn't turn out the way you thought they would. You still have a family who loves you, and who would do anything for you."

"What am I supposed to do now?"

"Whatever you want."

"I have a brother, Gideon. I don't even know him."

He sighed. "If you want to find him, I'll leave

Tristan in charge, and we'll search for him together."

"What about Hannah and Poppy, my sis—*cousins*. They chose me. They're depending on me. What if they're not omegas? I told them *everything*. They could get hurt."

He nodded. "That's what an alpha does, Amelia. She protects her family."

"Poppy is mated to Tristan. She'll be part of your pack soon enough."

"No, my love. They're not only my pack. You're my mate, therefore you're *their* alpha too. They're *our* pack. You and I are partners."

Amelia snorted. "You didn't treat me like your partner."

"I know."

"Gideon, if you ever lie to me again—"

"I *know*," he groaned.

"I hope you do know, because I won't forgive you a second time."

He nodded and pressed a kiss to her forehead. "I understand, my love."

"What about my aunt and uncle?"

"They raised you, Amelia. They might not have given birth to you, but you're still their daughter."

She sighed in defeat. "What if I can't figure out how to trust them again after this?"

"They protected you."

"They let me believe I was a mortal woman of the *Ton* with nothing but a marriage and children to occupy my life."

"*To keep you safe.*"

Amelia huffed. "Don't defend them. You're supposed to be on my side."

"I'm always on your side. I'm simply pointing out the facts. If you want to disown them that's your choice. I'll support it, but you will regret it, I promise you. They love you and just want the best for you. They have always had your sole interest at heart. If you can't forgive them, don't invite them to our wedding. But if you can find it in your heart to recognize what they were trying to do for you, then they deserve to be there."

"Are we still getting married?"

His grip tightened. "I didn't hear you call it off."

"I didn't."

"I certainly didn't."

"Then I guess we are," she said carefully.

He exhaled seemingly in relief, then immediately froze as the sound of footsteps grew near.

A long slow clap interrupted Amelia's moment of uncertainty. His scent hit her before she twisted to face the intruder. "Lord Cowen."

Lord Cowen rolled his eyes. "Touching as this is, I cannot allow it to continue. Amelia belongs to me, pup. Get your hands off her." He halted several feet from where they sat and stared down at them with fury in his eyes.

"Amelia is my mate," growled Gideon in confusion.

"Lord Cowen was with the rogues. He came to your house. He was the one who told me the truth about my parents," insisted Amelia as she got to her feet.

Gideon rose beside her and put himself between Amelia and Lord Cowen. "You had no right—"

"I have *every* right! I have worked too hard and followed her for too long to have an insolent little sprat like you steal her away. I'm the reason she's here! Without me she'd still be in Greenland with her brother!"

"Wait…" Amelia inhaled sharply. "What are you saying? You…you're the one who killed my parents?"

Lord Cowen groaned. "I honestly thought you were smarter than this! *Of course* it was me! *You* are not the one I wanted orginally. I wanted your mother, but plans change, accidents happen."

"You were in charge of the rogues," summarized Gideon.

"As much as anyone can be. Now that we've dispensed with the niceties, take your hands off my mate."

"She doesn't belong to you," insisted Gideon angrily.

"Her deceitful mother gave me hope that we would be together long before Victor Cavendash appeared. She betrayed me! She chose *him*. Rosalie owed me a bride! When they refused to hand you over, I decided to take matters into my own hands. Give me my due, boy!"

"You're a rogue, Cowen. Your due is a swift death," snapped Gideon.

"He knows where my brother is," insisted Amelia softly.

"You can't trust him, Melia." Gideon swore.

"He hasn't lied yet."

Lord Cowen smirked.

"He's a rogue, my love." Gideon turned and tugged her into his arms. "You can't leave with him."

"I would never. But he knows where I can find my brother."

"You want me to spare his life." Gideon groaned. "You don't understand what you're asking."

"Not spare. I want you to postpone his execution. He killed my parents. He kidnapped my sister. He terrorized all of London. I've lost as much as anyone to this bastard, but I need to know where my brother is. He's the only family I have left."

"You have me, Melia. You have my parents, my sisters, and your own family. You are not alone. We will find your brother, but not like this. Not with him."

Amelia opened her mouth to argue further, only to be interrupted by the sound of snarling. Her focus darted toward Lord Cowen, who was no longer a duke, but a large grizzled wolf with stained canines and mangy fur. Her heart leapt as the wolf stalked toward them, and Gideon instantly spun to face the threat, shielding her from the elder rogue once more.

"Melia, love...tell me you'll forgive me if I kill him," insisted Gideon carefully.

"But he knows—"

"Melia!" Gideon inched away from her, drawing the rogue's attention away from Amelia and toward himself.

"I might never find him, Gideon!"

"If I don't kill him, he's going to kill me, Melia."

"No, you're stronger than him, you can—"

"He's a rogue, Melia. There's no subduing him. He dies or I do. You're going to have to decide."

"Between you and my brother?"

The rogue leapt through the air, and took off at a dead run toward Gideon, forcing her mate to dive out of the way, where he hit the ground rolling. He lunged back up a few seconds later, but Lord Cowen was already racing toward him once more, knocking him off his feet and back onto the ground.

"Melia!"

Amelia swallowed. As much as she wanted to find her brother, there was no way she was losing Gideon to do so. "I will forgive you," vowed Amelia.

Gideon sighed. "Stay back."

The wolf spun and rushed toward Gideon. Cowan's fangs flashing dangerously in the sunlight as he made an attempt to maim her mate.

"Why aren't you changing, Gideon?" cried Amelia as the wolf spun and lunged at her mate once more.

"It's daylight. There are people around. Any of them could see us," explained Gideon breathlessly as he ducked to avoid another attack. "We can't risk exposing our people."

"He is!"

Gideon shook his head. "He's a *rogue*, Melia. That's the whole point!"

Amelia squealed in terror for her betrothed as Lord Cowen bolted back toward Gideon—his gaze filled with deadly intent. The wolf in her demanded to be released to protect their mate, but Amelia kept a careful leash on the beast. To shift now would reveal what she was and risk everyone she loved. But to remain in her human skin could mean losing Gideon forever. Her heart ached as she struggled to make a decision, and fresh fear soaked her body as tears streamed down her cheeks. She couldn't lose Gideon.

Her inner wolf howled in agreement, and Amelia prepared to shift into the beast, knowing all the while that it would mean having to leave London in order to protect those she called family. Gideon couldn't risk doing so—too many depended on him. Amelia accepted that she had to be the one. She closed her eyes in preparation for the change.

A single shot rang out, and everything went silent.

Shocked, Amelia straightened and spun on her heel to comprehend what had just happened. She was infinitely relieved to find Gideon standing several feet away—unharmed, but looking just as stunned as she felt. Between them, Lord Cowen lay dead at Gideon's feet.

"It has taken me years to track you down, sister. I wasn't about to lose you all over again to the likes of this bastard."

Amelia gasped and focused on the man responsible for the duke's untimely death. "Sister?"

The man grinned and tucked a double barrel flintlock pistol behind his back into a holster hanging from his hips. "Killian Cavendash. I believe we have much to discuss."

Chapter Fourteen

As if her day couldn't get any more outrageous, Amelia was on her way home with Gideon on one side, and her brother on the other, where they'd decided as a group that the best place to clear the air would be back at the Rochester townhouse. They'd just passed the Cavendash home when they managed to bump into the one person that could make things infinitely worse.

Gideon attempted to pull Amelia away, but it was too late. The damage was done.

"Well isn't this…interesting." Lady Walch snickered. "I don't recall receiving a wedding invitation, nor do I recall an engagement announcement. I'm sure my mother would *love* to hear about this!" Evangeline eyed Killian suspiciously but dismissed him to focus on Amelia instead.

Of course, the Lady of the Walch house— Evangeline's mother, *would* be the greatest gossip the *Ton* had ever seen.

The door to Amelia's house opened as if on cue, and Hadley stepped out. He glowered at Lady Walch and stepped between them as if to shield Amelia.

"Enough, Evangeline. It's been a long week. I'll walk you home." He glanced at Killian briefly, but like Evangeline, ultimately dismissed the new addition to their group.

"I can't be seen with you *in public*," hissed Lady

Walch. Her gaze darted down the street cautiously.

Amelia frowned. Something was going on here that she hadn't quite grasped yet.

"Can't you," growled Hadley.

Evangeline pierced him with a dark look.

"Are you…" Amelia wasn't sure she could even ask the question.

"Evangeline is a half-blood…and my mate," admitted Hadley hesitantly.

Astonished did not quite reflect how Amelia felt upon hearing Hadley's words. Of all the things she'd expected to hear, that was the *last*. "How long have you known?"

"Since the ball where you were supposed to announce your engagement."

Amelia nodded. "Right." Evangeline *had* been in attendance. The shrew had taunted Beatrix, and Amelia had nearly confronted her. She remembered now. It seemed like so long ago—had it really only been four days?

Gideon's gaze brightened. "That's *right*. I did give your father permission to buy that house across town. You'll be delighted to know that the rumors are true. Amelia is to be my wife before the season ends, and the female *alpha* of this territory."

He didn't say it, but Amelia recognized a threat when she heard one.

Evangeline swallowed—her face now a bit pale. "Congratulations," she mumbled.

"Thank you, we appreciate the gesture," said Gideon with a satisfied nod.

Hadley sighed. "Let me see you home, Evangeline. My coach is covered. No one will see us together."

Amelia watched them disappear into the stables behind Cavendash house.

"Thank you. You didn't need to defend me, but I appreciate you doing so."

"I have never liked her," admitted Gideon. "But it seems she is to join our family soon."

Amelia nodded. "We should try to welcome her." The words were bitter in her throat, but she meant each one. Hadley might not be her real brother, but he was as much her brother as Parker and the others. He was still family and part of her pack, at least until she married Gideon. Evangeline might not deserve her support, but Hadley did. If Evangeline was to be his bride, Amelia would try her best to get along with the nasty chit.

Chapter Fifteen

Amelia walked into Rochester house with her head held high. Her heart pounded with anxiety, but she didn't allow it to show. She managed a brave front as she and Gideon entered the dining room and found almost their entire family sitting around the table—as if they'd been expecting her.

"Lady Rochester," began Amelia immediately, addressing Gideon's mother first.

Gertrude Rochester stood and without a word walked toward them. She enveloped Amelia in a hug the instant she was close enough and held her tight for a moment. "Thank you for saving my life."

"I need to apologize for the way I acted."

"No, dear one. There's nothing to forgive. You had every right to question my motives. I'm glad you didn't hold back. You will make a beautiful alpha. My son is lucky to have you, and I'm fortunate as well." She pulled away, but kissed Amelia's forehead. "Roderick and I will be in the drawing room if you need us."

Gideon's father immediately got to his feet and followed his mate out of the room, brushing past Killian, who leaned nonchalantly against the doorframe watching the entire thing unfold.

Amelia inhaled as she attempted to gather her courage. She had no idea what she would say to her parents, but she couldn't leave things as they were.

"Hannah and I will be in the garden," announced Poppy, as if sensing her distress, and with Tristan in tow the three of them exited toward the kitchen.

Parker cleared his throat and headed toward her.

Amelia expected the worst, but he simply hugged her.

"You've always been my sister, and you always will be. If you need anything, you know where to find me."

She nodded and watched him leave as well before taking a seat at the table across from her parents.

"Do you want me to leave?" asked Gideon.

She shook her head. "No. You can stay. We don't have any secrets. I'll likely tell you everything anyway, so we might as well make this simple."

Gideon nodded and took the seat next to her, then reached beneath the table and pulled her hand into his for support.

"Where's Lizbeth?" she asked finally.

"She is asleep in Gideon's sister's room," said Lady Cavendash softly, referring to one of the twins who'd married the year before in a dramatic double wedding. Her curious gaze darted toward Killian, but she said nothing.

Amelia swallowed and motioned for Killian to join them. Where to begin? "I don't know…where to go from here. You might have lied to me, but you also took me into your home and raised me as your own. You treated me the same way you treated Hannah, Poppy, and Lizbeth. For that I will always love you. You didn't have to do that, but you did. Thank you."

"Amelia—" Henry Cavendash opened his mouth to interrupt.

"Let me finish." Amelia swallowed again. This next part was going to be hard. "I'm not content with things as they are. I want to know about my father, my *birth* father. *And* my mother. I'm going to stay here with Gideon. Hannah and Poppy can stay too and chaperone so as to protect my reputation and Hannah's as well, if that's what *they* want. Mama…" Amelia smiled empathetically as her mother dragged in a shaky breath. "You're welcome to plan our wedding, and you're both welcome to attend. I hope you will, and I'm sorry for what I said. I didn't mean any of it."

Her mother swiped at a tear as it slid silently down her own cheek—her focus on Amelia now, rather than the stranger who now sat quietly at the end of the table.

"We're sorry we hurt you. We never meant to. My brother loved you with all his heart, know that. We've never thought of you as anything less than our daughter. You were our first girl, and a new experience for us. We thought keeping you girls from knowing the truth would make things easier for you. Life is hard enough without being a shifter. I hope you can forgive us," explained her father gently. He glanced at Killian and tears welled in his eyes. "I know who you are."

Killian inhaled sharply.

"Papa, this is Killian—my brother."

Lord Cavendash nodded. "I know." He swiped at his tears. "You look just like our Amelia."

"And you look just like the paintings my mother kept of our father," admitted Killian softly.

Henry Cavendash groaned. "I tried to save him."

Amelia felt new tears spill down her cheeks as he spoke of her father.

"What happened?" asked Killian. "I've always

thought he abandoned me. I was a grown man before my aunt told me Amelia existed."

Henry Cavendash shook his head. "No. He loved you both very much." He sucked in a deep breath. "You were just babies when it happened. I had never even met you yet, but that night…everything about that night felt off. I had trouble sleeping, and it was as if I just knew something horrible was happening. They arrived in the middle of the night in the pouring rain, and there was so much blood…" He sobbed. "He said it was safer to keep you apart. He didn't want the rogues to find you. Your father left me the address of the home where he'd left you and I had thought to send for you one day, but it never seemed like the right time. I should have. I'm so sorry."

Amelia was practically bawling by the time her father finished speaking, and her heart broke all over again.

"Thank you," managed Killian with a sad smile. "I've spent so much of my life hating them. No one has ever told me the truth. If there's anything I can do to repay you—"

"Stay. Amelia needs you."

Amelia's tear-filled gaze darted toward her father.

"Isn't London occupied territory?" asked Killian.

"It is," agreed Gideon. "As I said before, we would be honored if you stayed. In fact…I would be honored if you would be my best man. I intend to marry your sister, and I know she'd love to have you there."

Amelia twisted and wrapped her arms around Gideon's shoulders, too emotional to articulate a proper response.

He hugged her back without hesitation.

"If you don't mind my asking, how did you find us?" asked Lord Cavendash roughly.

Amelia pulled away from Gideon to focus on her brother.

Killian shifted in his seat. "I wasn't looking for you. I was looking for my father. I wanted to confront him. I was hiding out on the outskirts of London to avoid being caught within the territory borders, in that graveyard where I shot the rogue."

Amelia's parents turned to stare at each other in surprise.

"Lord Cowen," acknowledged Amelia. "He was the rogue who killed our parents."

"I saw you that night with him." Killian nodded toward Gideon in emphasis. "And somehow I just knew you were my sister. I've been trying to figure out a way to meet you ever since, but most alphas tend to kill invaders, especially lone wolves with no pack to speak of their reputation. I've been living in the graveyard, hoping you'd come back and I could speak to you."

"Edgar Cowen?" asked Henry in confusion. "I don't understand."

"He was originally from our mother's pack. He was interested in our mother and felt betrayed when she married our father," explained Amelia with a sigh. She dried her cheeks and cleared her throat. "He demanded compensation for the loss of her hand, but when my parents refused to hand me over, Lord Cowen and his pack of rogues chased them across the country. He's been stalking me ever since. He was behind all of this."

Lord Cavendash swore. "He's dead now though?"

Gideon nodded. "He attacked us in the graveyard this morning. Killian shot him."

"At least there's that," growled Henry.

"And the other rogues? The ones who killed that girl and took Lizbeth?" asked Amelia.

"They are dead. We took care of them in Glasgow," explained Henry.

"It's all finally over?" asked Amelia, not entirely convinced she could believe it.

"Not completely." Gideon offered her a hopeful grin. "I believe a wedding is in order."

"You are absolutely right!" Amelia pursed her lips thoughtfully. "But then again, I might change my mind."

The look of stunned disbelief and appalled horror on her beloved's face had Amelia bending forward with giggles of amusement. Before she could catch her breath, Gideon abruptly yanked her chair closer to his until the profile of her body rested against his knees, and whispered suggestively in her ear, "You my little she-wolf are going to pay for those words."

His threats were like molten lava, setting every nerve in her body on fire, and Amelia faced him as she spoke. "Turnabout is fair play, mate," she warned innocently.

His response came in the form of a physical assault on her lips, right there in front of everyone, that had her family clearing their throats and quickly exiting the room.

Amelia dissolved into giggles once more, and he wrapped his arms around her, drawing her body onto his lap. Not many could say their lover made them feel the way Gideon made her feel, and she knew she was fortunate to have him.

She sobered as his gaze raked over her face fervently, and Amelia leaned forward to kiss him once more, lured by his heat. She was certainly looking forward to spending the rest of her life with her wolf.

A word about the author...

Born in Georgetown, Ohio, Cassidee Meeks makes her home in a small town in Eastern Kentucky where she spends her days with her husband, wrangling her kids and all the stray cats her family will allow.

You might find her tending chickens in her back yard, or with her nose buried in a good book, but most times, Cassidee can be found deep in her writing cave where she spends her evenings arguing with fictional characters, who inevitably get their way and their stories told.

Thank you for purchasing
this publication of The Wild Rose Press, Inc.

For questions or more information
contact us at
info@thewildrosepress.com.

The Wild Rose Press, Inc.
www.thewildrosepress.com

Lightning Source UK Ltd.
Milton Keynes UK
UKHW021451070720
366156UK00014B/1453

9 781509 231348